The call of the road

THE CALL OF THE ROAD

WILHELM WILLEKE

Title The Call of the Road
ISBN: 9789564018799
Stamp: Independently published
All right reserved
Copyright © 2020 Wilhelm Willeke
Cover and Back Cover design: Dragonbookcovers.com
Translation: Nathaly López Cruz
Layout: César López Yauzá

Somewhere in this book, there is a phrase waiting for you to make sense of your existence.

Anonymous

Table of contents

PREFACE

T like any other.   And it is not that it is not his book is not a thriller and adventure novel because throughout its pages we do not find adventures and suspense in large doses, since the truth is that it is full of them from beginning to end, but because it is something else. It is a song to freedom and, above all, a passionate declaration of love for life on the road. Wilhelm Willeke, the author of this thrilling thriller, lends Daniel, his alter ego in the novel, some features that are peculiar to him, so that although the adventures narrated in it are fictional, its protagonist keeps a certain kinship with reality. From a very young age, Willeke showed an extraordinary restlessness that led him to travel around the world. His adventurous character is evident in the fact that, like his character, he has never had much trouble getting to an airport and catching the first plane available, no matter what the destination. One of his greatest hobbies, which has marked not only his personal life but also his work life, is his attraction to the sea—which is also reflected in some chapters of this book—a hobby that led him to found a diving school, which he owns and teaches, and to dive into the waters of a number of countries, including Indonesia, Thailand, Belize, the Dominican Republic, El Salvador, Mexico, Peru, Guatemala, Honduras and his native Chile. But the closest connection to his character is the love they both feel, one in reality and the other in fiction, for the world of motorcycles. Like Daniel, Willeke discovered this fascinating universe, albeit belatedly, but once he tried it out, his spirit was imbued with that inexplicable desire

— we could almost say, need — to get out on the road;

with that almost magical feeling that takes hold of some motorcycles and never abandons them again.

Those who have never ridden a motorbike may find it difficult to understand the hypnotic sensation of having before them that infinite line of leaden color that gets lost in the horizon, as if swallowed by the clouds, and that can lead anyone who knows how to follow it to any place in the world. But the road is not only that, it is also its smells, its sounds, the nature it crosses. And its skies. Although the character in the novel, perhaps a bit like Willeke himself, has a bit of a lone wolf about him, he feels, like any asphalt rider who really is one, a fraternal bond with his biker brothers, with those who share with him a passion for the irresistible and attractive world of the road. One of these "sisters of the road" is Camila, an enigmatic biker whom the protagonist meets by chance and with whom he ends up sharing his adventures. Both are very similar and think that whoever has not ever traveled the world on two wheels does not know what freedom is.

Wilhelm Willeke masterfully transports us through the pages of this novel to a world brimming with sensations in which, together with the main characters of those, pursued by a fearsome threat, we can travel the roads of Chile and Argentina, taste the immense and splendid skies, the steep peaks of the Andes and be surprised, while bathing in a majestic lake, by the furious eruption of a terrifying volcano. And it is possible that this novel, in addition to keeping its readers tense from the first to the last page, will also make some of them feel, deep inside, the call of the road.

[11

]

CHAPTER 1

Hand cursed the first package inwardly. From e felt a small sting in the back of his left hand the day he received it, he had only been gloved in his right hand because the doctor had advised him to keep the spider's bite aired. What on earth would the fourth packet contain? He tried to turn his thoughts away from it and concentrated on the majestic expanse of sky before him, barely speckled in its upper layers by the tiny white spots of some lost cirrus in the midst of so much blue. Whoever has never travelled the world on two wheels, knows not what freedom is, thought Daniel as he gave his Midnight Star petrol, which he felt firmly under his legs, and was grateful for the air that beat strongly against his face on that torrid summer morning. He wore his visor up to cool himself off a little, because the road increased the heat of the season and his throat began to feel dry. Even so, he enjoyed every second of the ride; he had become so attached to the bike that he could no longer conceive of life without it. He inhaled deeply the smell of the bushes and the pines that splashed left and right the lands that bordered that dark and wonderful line that stretched out in front of him as far as the eye could see, as if he were going to get lost in the infinite: the road. How had he come to love so much that fragment of dusty asphalt on which he was now riding as a free ride on his machine? It was almost by chance. All his life he had been an adventurous person, perhaps a little thoughtless because he was convinced that spontaneity was part of adventure. It didn't cost him anything to go to an airport and take the first plane available, no matter what the destination; the crucial thing was that it would take him

[12]

far away, as if those remote and unknown places were calling him from a distance, claiming his presence. But air was not the only means to discover new unexplored areas. He had also become a diving instructor and had immersed himself in the deep waters of a blue ocean on countless occasions, in search of exotic landscapes and mysterious shipwrecks. It seemed as if he always had to live his life on the edge, exploring the possibilities it offered, expanding his spirit beyond the boundaries of that world in which he lived, and which always seemed to remain small. But a strange day came when, almost imperceptibly at first, and more quickly as time went by, everything began to lose its meaning; the trips no longer motivated him, and he felt that even improvisation no longer had that captivating charm that had guided his steps until then. What had happened? Perhaps his soul had been filled with so many experiences that it had ended up exhausting his illusion? He was barely thirty—four years old and already felt old, as if he had come back from everything. Then his mother's death came upon him like a sledgehammer, and he felt as if that blow had taken away the last living fragment of his soul. He wandered around for a long time without a fixed destination until a friend suggested that they take a trip together on a motorbike, which Daniel reluctantly agreed to, more to please his friend than out of genuine interest. But things went wrong here too: his friend, Mario, found out he was going to be a father and cancelled the trip at the last minute. However, a little out of inertia, Daniel continued with the idea. He bought himself a magnificent Yamaha and set off without a second thought, just like in the old days, without a fixed destination, abandoning himself to the whim of fate. "And why not,' thought Daniel now, as the sound of his girl's engine caressed his ears, destiny brings you a gift at the most unexpected

[13

]

moment. He had been offered two: the motorbike he was leaning over at the time and the road. That was almost a year ago and he had never regretted, not even for a single moment, that he had decided to continue the journey alone, because, although he did not know it yet, the journey he had undertaken that day was not just one more of the many he had begun throughout his life, but a journey that was to transform his life completely.

The impact of a mosquito on his sunglasses tore him away from those thoughts that had kept him away for a few moments from the one that haunted him all the time in his head. He felt uneasy about the damn package. It was his fourth in a month, though this time it was to be delivered by hand. The sun was getting hotter and hotter, and the temperature was already over thirty degrees. He was alone several miles south of Santiago and had rolled down that road a thousand times. Not far from there was the roadhouse where he had been summoned, where in addition to quenching his thirst he could put an end to that absurd game. I didn't know who would give him up or what he would look like, but I didn't think I could let him go without giving him an explanation.

When he arrived, he stopped the bike next to several trucks that were parked. The face of his watch informed him that it was still ten minutes to twelve, so he amused himself by gazing with pleasure at the glow that the sun was shining on the polished forms of a formidable tanker. The tank, as well as the chassis and the cab, were bright yellow, and his gaze was caught on its shiny surface like a fly in a spider's web. Its owner must have spent hours polishing it. Compared to the muddy or dusty cabs and trailers of the other trucks, it looked like a showpiece. For some reason, which he could not identify, he found the contrast disturbing. He looked at the huge tyres and they were intact, not a speck of dust, as if someone had placed them there without the road having rolled. Suddenly, a lizard dodged its boots and hid behind a heat—drying bush. He followed it with his eyes and could see something beyond, a group of motorcycles arranged in a row and resting like saddles beside a watering hole. He approached them and looked at them for a while. Would one of those bikers be the one to make the delivery? He immediately dismissed the idea because, although he knew it made no sense, he found it hard to associate a biker with anything sordid, since for him being a road rider was synonymous with generosity. He was fascinated by the world of the road, a universe with its own rules, full of peculiarities and nuances, which until he frequented it himself had gone unnoticed. He breathed in the torrid morning air, and from somewhere came the unmistakable smells of that magnificent and untamed universe: dust, asphalt, the distant stench of some dead animal, the reheated leaf litter and the sap of an old tree wounded by the sun. As soon as he crossed the threshold of the premises, he noticed the change in temperature and liked the atmosphere, which was somewhat charged with tobacco smoke and frying — because it was cooler and more welcoming than the dryness outside. An old Bon Jovi song was playing, and its chords mixed with the lazy hum of the fan blades hanging from the ceiling. The first thing he did was look around the crowd, but he found nothing unusual about the parishioners: people on the road cooling their throats on a hot day, nothing more. Nor did he get the impression that anyone was particularly attentive to his presence, so he sat down on a stool by the wooden bar, in keeping with the rustic style of the bar, and ordered a cold beer, while waiting for the arrival of the stranger with whom he had arranged to meet. The waitress she had seen there on other

[15
]

occasions was not there. He regretted it because, as he remembered, she was a nice girl with an easy smile and a pleasant conversation. The bartender who served him, however, was an unassuming fellow who hardly looked at him. He was entertained by watching them play billiards at one of the tables at the back of the room. The coolness of the amber liquid bubbled up on his palate before gently descending down his throat, moisturizing it. The alcohol revived her chest a bit and she immediately felt in good spirits. But it was short—lived, for the gloomy thoughts that had accompanied him that morning prevailed again. What disturbed man could do such a thing, and for what? He took another drink from his bottle and his mind went back to a few weeks ago when he received the first package in his house. It had no return address, and when he opened it, he immediately let go of it when he saw something moving inside. A huge brownish spider came out of the box at full speed. Daniel didn't expect it and found it difficult to catch the animal, because when it was free, it moved incredibly fast on its many legs to try to escape. He managed to catch it again in the box and closed it with difficulty, not before receiving a sting in his left hand that burned as if acid had been thrown at it. He would return that magnificent specimen of arachnid to the mountain, where it should never have left. He took it as a bad joke, although in his heart he felt it to be something disturbing, even threatening. A week later, he received a new package of the same size and characteristics as the previous one, the same brown brown wrapping paper sealed with a plastic strip. He opened it with some caution, hoping that some live animal would come out again, but this time he found the small carcass of a chicken. At first, he thought it had drowned on the way, but he soon realized that its throat had been cut before it was sent. The third package arrived a couple of weeks later. This time it was full of something that looked like chocolate figures to him at first, but then he identified it as a bunch of insects, some living and some dead, struggling anxiously in a shapeless mass inside that little coffin. He was racking his brains all the time, making hundreds of guesses as to who might have sent him these gifts and whether they contained any message. He considered giving an account of it to the police, but eventually he dismissed the idea, he was not sure that such things could be covered up by crime. At last, after four weeks, a letter arrived, also without a sender, in which, with a neat but unknown calligraphy, he was summoned the next day at twelve o'clock in the morning to a roadhouse next to a petrol bomb. It was a remote place, in the middle of nowhere. Daniel knew it because he had stopped to refuel his motorbike and had taken the opportunity to have a drink and talk to the waitress for a while. In that place, according to the text, the last package would be delivered to him and he would finally understand the reason for the deliveries.

And there I was, in that bar, following the instructions of a stranger. Suddenly he felt like an idiot and took a long drink from the bottle to get the thought out of his head.

—Hey, buddy, you want to join us?

He turned to where the voice was coming from. Sitting at a table three men and a woman looked at him. From the look of them, he soon realized that they were the owners of the motorcycles he had seen parked outside.

—Of course! —he replied with a smile and headed towards them.

Could they be the ones in the package? It didn't have to be that way. It is not at all strange that a biker should invite another biker to share a beer, even if they do not

[17

]

know each other at all.   If there was one thing he had learned in that last year, it was the spirit of the pack that binds bikers together. There is something that somehow unites them, and it is not only the spirit of adventure or the desire for freedom, but the medium in which they move: the road. They are all citizens of that small cosmos and they take care of each other, especially because on the road they will find many more people moving around on four wheels than on two, and sometimes the former is a danger to the latter. At first, this bond between strangers had surprised him, and reminded him a little of the behavior of the Tuaregs in the desert, whose hospitality is legendary. He had realized that the road was a similar environment, large areas of land, sometimes lonely, where one could need help at any time. A whole world with its own rules. For example, if someone is in trouble, he puts his helmet on the ground; that's enough for no biker to pass by. He also learned the peculiar gesture of greeting each other as they crossed the road, releasing his gloved hand from the handlebars and placing it at knee level to form a V with the index and middle fingers. It doesn't matter if they know each other or not, because, in reality, even if they haven't seen each other in life, in some deep way, which someone who is not a motorcyclist cannot understand, all those who ride their machines on the asphalt are family. Many of them are lone wolves, but they know that their comrades are somewhere on the asphalt. No one on two wheels is really alone on the road.

In time he realized that every single motorcycle he had ever known had its own story, a pain or a desire, that had driven them to take to the road. As he headed for the table, he wondered what the peculiar story of those four would be.

—One hot morning," he said by way of greeting, as he took his seat.

—You can say that again, my friend," replied the one who looked like the oldest of them, a guy in his forties, with a graying beard and a distant Mapuche air on his face, who toasted his beer bottle with Daniel's. And that was just the beginning!

—Daniel," he said by way of introduction, as he lit a cigarette and breathed in with delight the smoke that tickled his lungs.

—Nice to meet you, I'm Oscar. These are Camila, Tomás and El Cholo," he introduced his companions, who responded with a gesture of greeting as they were named. They were all dressed similarly, like Daniel himself, for this was the usual attire of the motorcyclists: leather jackets, jeans and high boots, although the jackets now hung on the backs of the chairs.

They talked for a while amicably with rock and roll in the background. The conversation revolved around their life on the road, which was the recurring conversation between motorcyclists, or their machines: about engine capacity, stability, power. Oscar and Camila exchanged their experiences on the road with Daniel, but Tomás, a much younger blond guy, ended up taking over the conversion. His friends seemed to know him and let him talk, so the boy went on about his adventures on his Kawasaki. He was so excited that the words came rushing out of his mouth, as if he were a proud father praising his little boy. As he listened, Daniel looked from time to time at the door to see if anyone came in, but his eyes ended up on the girl, this Camila. You couldn't say she was a dazzling beauty, but she was pretty and had beautiful eyes. He noticed the peculiarity of that bluish iris, it was full of opaline reflections that he had never seen on the surface of the earth, only rarely on reefs under the sea. She attended Thomas' passionate conversation with amusement.

Suddenly, Daniel had the feeling that he was being stared at as well. He turned his gaze to the side and his eyes met those of the Cholo. He was the only one of the four who hadn't said a word since he sat down. He would have been about his age, or perhaps a couple of years older, and had a somewhat gaunt face with sharp features. Under his tight—fitting shirt was a thin but compact torso. His gaze seemed petrified on his face, as if some alienated god had chiseled it away in those moments by denying him movement. Something similar was happening with her mouth: under a black moustache, her lips were pressed almost exaggeratedly in a gesture of tension. The ember of her lit cigarette, which seemed to be caught like a prey in a trap in those motionless lips, was slowly consumed, while its smoke crossed the face of the Cholo like the ectoplasm of a ghost. Although he had surprised him by looking at it, he didn't look away, and that caused Daniel a feeling of strangeness and also a certain uneasiness. He didn't quite know how to react to what was clearly strange behavior, but then he realized that perhaps he was the person who had summoned him there. Finally, he said to himself, now you'll tell me what the hell is going on here. As she was about to start talking, she felt a hand resting on her shoulder and she instinctively turned a little abruptly at that unexpected contact. The waiter, who had touched him, drew back a little surprised by his reaction.

—Excuse me," he said somewhat self—consciously, as he extended his hand towards Daniel to hand him a small package. For you.

Daniel stood up from his chair and stared at the waiter as he took the package.

[20
]

—A man gave it to me... He said it was for you..." repeated the waiter somewhat frightened by the tense attitude of that customer.

—Where is it? —I don't know. —asked this one, looking all over the place.

—He's gone," said the waiter.

—Shit! —exclaimed Daniel, as he reached into his pockets for a ticket to pay.

—You're invited, mate," exclaimed Oscar, winking at him and raising his beer as a toast.

—Thank you! —replied Daniel, waving his thumb up in gratitude and taking his jacket from the back of the chair to leave the premises in a hurry.

When he came out, the sun hit him hard in the face and the light blinded him momentarily. He took the dark glasses from his jacket pocket and put them on. He looked back and forth but saw no movement. However, his expert biker's gaze detected some dust floating in the dense air heated by the action of the sun's rays on the ground, and since he was not blowing any air at all, he knew that he must have been lifted recently by some moving vehicle. He looked more closely around and then he realized: the yellow tanker was gone. He swore to himself, thinking he had been negligent. If he hadn't spent so much time talking to those bikers... He looked at the package in his hands. His heart skipped a beat. Would he find the answer to that nonsense inside? He threw his cigarette butt on the ground and stepped on the ember with his boot. Then he opened the package slowly, as if he was in no hurry to know its contents, or perhaps, as if he didn't really want to know. A bad feeling crossed his mind as he tore off the adhesive tape and pulled away the brown paper covering it. He thought it could be anything. Bugs? Some dead animal? But no matter how many things he imagined; it would never have occurred to him what he found when he opened it.

CHAPTER 2

He took the pictures that the box contained and looked at them one by one without being able to understand what that could mean and what relationship it had with the previous packages. One after the other, those photographs showed him in his intimacy, in his home, sleeping in his bed, lying on the sofa. There was even one in which he appeared dozing on the armchair in front of the television with an empty beer in his hand... In none of them was he awake and they had been taken over the last few years, probably since he moved from his parents' house to his apartment when he was twenty—two. But he didn't remember ever having had them done. The only person in all the photographs was him, and they gave the impression that he was completely alone. He examined them carefully over and over again. Some were color snapshots; others were black and white. The paper was either matt or glossy, and on the surfaces, especially in the corners, you could see that the paper had been worn away by time. The detail with which they had been taken shook him. The closeness of the shots, the framing of his face... were so close and so intimate that you could even smell his sweat, hear his snoring, read his dreams... Throughout the series, the changes that had taken place over the years were evident, both in him and in his apartment, and as he looked at them again, a suspicion was taking shape in his head. But that could not be. It was simply impossible. The sun began to become intolerable because its rays impacted directly on him. He circled the bar, seeking refuge in the shadow cast by the south—facing back. A cow nibbling on a dry bush raised her head to look at him only curiously and returned to her bush, wiping away some buzzing flies with her tail. Daniel wondered what a cow was doing loose in such a barren place in the middle of nowhere. He looked at the photos again. He had less and less doubts: someone had taken them while he was not aware of it. But who could have done that? The idea that someone had been invading his privacy and spying on his most intimate moments during the last few years made him dizzy and he had to lean against the wall because he got a little dizzy. He took a deep breath and spent a few seconds with his eyes closed and his head on his shoulder. A thousand images passed through his mind in which he saw himself unconscious, defenseless, helpless, from a perspective in which he was at once a spectator and an exhibited object, an observer and an observed. He looked up and saw his hand resting on the peeling surface of the wall: the spider's bite seemed to have grown and was somewhat redder. From a skylight that opened a little higher up on the wall came the metallic whine of the Guns N' Roses guitar playing inside. Because of the vague stench coming from it, he thought it must have hit the laundry room.

I couldn't stop looking at the pictures. No one other than someone in his inner circle could have done that, but the idea terrified him. How was that possible? Someone in his family? His friends? His ex—girlfriend? And how had they gotten into his house so many times without him noticing? As he thought about it, more questions came up. But what struck him most was the thought of what might go through the mind of someone who had done something like this. He couldn't be a normal person. Someone cold—blooded enough to break into someone else's house, sneaking around, watching, keeping an eye on things. For years. For what purpose? He felt like he was naked, and a chill ran

[25

]

through his body. He rubbed his arms instinctively with his hands, as if to wipe the stranger's gaze clean, as if it were attached to his skin. The first thing that occurred to him was to go home and search everything, call his friends, interrogate them, but he soon changed his mind. He didn't want to leave the road. Now he felt more at home there, in his world of asphalt. What was strange to him at the time was his apartment, his home, that place where, in reality, he had never been alone without knowing it.

—Everything OK?

He looked up from the photos and directed them to the person who had spoken those words. He smiled.

—Well, I've been better," he said with a smile, and instinctively put the pictures in the box to hide them from the girl's view.

—You've come out of it. As if the devil were chasing you

—observed Camila, smiling at him in turn.

—The devil," he repeated. It was more like it was out here, waiting for me.

—In there? —she joked, pointing at the box.

—Yes, I caught him. Now he can't get out.

Camila laughed heartily and Daniel felt surprisingly relieved, as if her laughter had managed to dispel the dark clouds that had formed in his head for a few moments. The girl approached the cow and gently stroked its spotted back without the animal leaving her concentration in the bush.

—I see that you have met Clarita.

—It seems so," he said, taking the pack of cigarettes out of his pocket and offering Camila a cigarette.

—No, thanks," she refused. Then he looked at the cow and added, while still caressing it: "Do you know that cows always look north?

What's that? —asked Daniel, lighting his cigarette and giving it a deep puff.

—They seem to have sensors in their heads which enable them to recognize the Earth's magnetic field.

He looked at the girl with curiosity. Then he let the smoke slowly escape from his lungs, while he took off his sunglasses to see Camila's eyes better. She continued talking, as if for herself, while she continued to caress Clarita.

—She's connected to Mother Nature. We all are, but some animals do it in ways we don't even suspect. If we could see the world as they see it, we might be in for a surprise.

Daniel was fascinated by Camila's words. He asked her funny question:

—And how does a biker girl like you know these things?

—You see," she smiled again.

—What's a cow doing here? Camila shrugged.

—I see her sometimes. She must be running away from some farm in the interior.

—To a roadhouse? I like this cow. I'm sure she comes for the beer.

Camila laughed again and Daniel stared at her. The reflections of the sun managed to reveal even more nuances in her eyes than she had seen inside the premises.

—You come here a lot, then," said Daniel.

—Yes, often.

Suddenly Daniel had the same feeling again, which he had experienced inside the room, when he felt that someone was watching him.

—That cow would make a good steak on my plate.

Daniel and Camila looked out of the window. The one who had said that was the Cholo, who was looking out from there with a crooked smile under his moustache. Then he ran his tongue over his lips as if licking himself at a succulent morsel. Camila looked away in disgust, but Daniel kept looking at her. The Cholo extended his smile a little longer and disappeared.

—A strange man, your friend.

—He's not my friend.

—He thought... they were having a drink together.

—I'm with Oscar and Tomas. We invited him to sit with us, just like you. You know...

—Yes, biker camaraderie. —Daniel saw Camila caressing the cow again. Her brown hair was glowing in the sun. Poor Clarita.

—You look a bit like her..." said the girl with a hint of sadness in her voice.

—Me?" Daniel was surprised.

—I mean... I think you're a lonely person...

Daniel continued to look at the marine reflections in the girl's eyes in daylight. His thoughts suddenly settled, not knowing how, on Benjamin, his older brother.

—Lonely... —he repeated.

Then he felt the wound on his left— The sky stretched out before his eyes as if it were a huge blue— winged butterfly flying towards immensity. The clouds, white as freshly washed, piled up on the horizon in puffy cumulus clouds, adopting curious shapes, which evolved with the whim hand sting again, and as he brought his mind to it, he felt the box he was holding and seemed to burn even more than the bite.

—I have to go,' he said.

—I won't have you...

—No, no. It's just that I have to do things.

Good. I'll stay with Clarita," she said kissing the cow's head, which was up in those moments and looking towards where Daniel was, that is, towards the north. On second thought, maybe it wouldn't be so bad with a little ketchup.

Daniel looked at her somewhat perplexed.

—Will we see each other? —I wanted to know before he left.

—Sure," she smiled. On the road.

[29

]

CHAPTER 3

D on aniel was back on the road, riding his bike. The smells, the rumor of the wind, the sun on his face, the speed, the asphalt. That was his habitat and he had always felt safe there. But now the world seemed to him to be a more disturbing place, even those open spaces that he loved so much seemed to darken and hide some threat. As he went along, the white stripes painted on the roadway rushed towards him, giving the impression of spears hurling little men at him from under the pavement. His head was still spinning with the same idea: those pictures and the person who had taken them. But now, on the bike, he was thinking better. He was a man of action, restless, he had never liked to stop too long anywhere, and it seemed as if the thoughts came more clearly to his mind when he himself was in motion. He had very little information: a handwritten letter with careful calligraphy, three absurd packages with sordid contents, and a series of photographs that had been taken of him over the years without his noticing. Once again it crossed his mind to go to the police, but again he dismissed it. He didn't have enough facts and the story seemed implausible. But, above all, I didn't want to alert him, the guy who had taken the time and trouble to photograph him for years for some reason that only he knew. He feared that a police investigation would scare him off, that he might not even get in touch with him again. If this stranger, whoever he was, had spent years on the prowl, not feeling the need to make his existence known while spying on him, there was nothing to stop him, just as he had suddenly decided to come out of that long silence, from now plunging back in. She didn't want to push him

[30

]

away, she needed him to get in touch with her again, because that was the quickest way, perhaps the only way, to find out what the hell was going on. A bitter smile spread across his face for a moment, bathed in the warm air of the road; he found it ironic to think that his greatest ally at that time, the only one who could really help him unravel that mystery, was his own enemy. Suddenly he realized that he had just given that stranger a name. For the past few weeks he had mentally labeled him "that weird guy" or "the guy with the packages"; now he saw him differently, as his enemy. She also realized that she had always thought of him as a man, assuming that he was a man. But in reality, he could also be a woman. It could be anyone in his immediate environment, someone he trusted, someone he even loved. That thought increased his restlessness, and he tried to put it out of his mind, while trying to concentrate on driving.

It had been a long time since any vehicle had passed him; he had chosen a secondary road on which there was hardly any traffic. The good thing about moving around on a motorbike was that you were free to go anywhere, without having to plan anything or negotiate with anyone else, as is often the case when travelling on four wheels. The only restrictions you had to submit to were fuel and your own will. He could travel great distances in any direction and in a short time and deviate his path by the simple desire to do so, taking one path or another, without giving explanations to anyone, at random, without even needing to know his own destination. But this time he knew perfectly well where he was going. There was a small hut lost among the trees and bushes a few miles away, in a south—westerly direction, which at one time should have served as a warehouse, but now it was abandoned. It was occasionally frequented by some motorcyclists to rest, although most of the time it was empty, as it was not easily accessible, and few people knew it. He would go there when he needed to be alone, and that was one of those occasions. The road was flanked by old trees that cast a soft shadow over the road, and there, far from the main road, the sound of the engine was confused with the silence of the road, as if he and his bike were merging with nature.

I think you're a lonely man... That phrase emerged again... tingling through the tangle of thoughts in his head. Next to her, a pleasant image was formed, which for a second drove the discomfort from her mind: the opal iridescence of Camila's eyes. There was something special about that girl. And she seemed to have an instinct. They had barely exchanged a few words in a banal conversation, and she had perceived in him something that lay far below the surface, and which he thought was hidden from the view of others. Was it so obvious? Yes, he thought, he was a loner. But he hadn't always been like that. In fact, he had been comfortable with people from a very young age and had even been the leader of his gang as a teenager. But since Benjamin had left, all that had changed. Why had his older brother come to mind when Camila uttered those words? Did his disappearance have anything to do with his progressive isolation from the world, with that need to live his life without being tied to anything or anyone? Perhaps. He had always felt very close to Benjamin, for him he was not only his brother and best friend, but also the mirror in which he looked at himself, the smartest, strongest, nicest guy. And then suddenly that accident. Daniel felt his throat dry; the effect of the fresh beer seemed to have worn off. He was irritable and instinctively gave the bike more power. Sometimes he felt as if he and his machine were just one, as if his mood, his feelings, were transmitted through the cables, through the chassis, through the tyres... Or as if the current from the motor also electrified his muscles and nerves or the petrol ran through his veins. It had been a long time since he had thought about the death of his mother or the disappearance of his brother. His Yamaha had saved him, pulled him out of frustration. It had not only allowed him to escape physically from the world and to speed away from monotony, giving him all the territories, he could reach with his eyes, but it had also kept him away from bitter thoughts, from the feeling of loss. On the back of his girl he saw the world differently, from another angle. The very name of his bike, midnight star, was the perfect metaphor for what it had meant to him: a star in the middle of the night sky, far from everything, free, powerful and bright. But that package had brought him back to the past, and with him to the dark thoughts. Everyone thought their brother was dead. His car fell into the sea from a very high cliff. They didn't find the body, but they did find a few crates of beer in the back seat. Everything pointed to him having had a few too many and he must have lost control of the car. Diving teams combed the area for the body, but the ocean currents could have swept him out to sea. After a long and fruitless search, the police declared the case closed and he was officially considered dead, but both he and his mother refused to believe that Benjamin had been eaten by the fishes. Something told them that he could have swum, that he could have been saved, and that perhaps he had lost his memory or was in some unconscious hospital. But as the months and years passed, expectations had faded. He was the only one who still had a faint hope that he and his older brother would one day get back together, but by now she was as small as a tiny drop of water lost in the vastness of the ocean. An ocean whose waters he had explored countless times, perhaps with the intention of questioning the depths of the sea, in the vain hope of finding something in its vastness that would offer him a clue as to where his brother was.

Suddenly he felt a twist in his chest. His eyes had been fixed on a vehicle driving in the opposite direction to him. Again, the yellow glint caught his eye like the hypnotic pupils of a snake. The tanker was there, just a hundred and fifty meters from him, as if from nowhere. He clenched his fists firmly on the handlebars and continued his journey, slowing down a little as he approached. When he got close enough, he tried to spot the driver in the cabin, but all he could make out was a shadow behind the reflection of the sun on the glass. As he drove past, he noticed that the surface of the tank glowed like the tail of a rare reptile. He thought again of the strange delicacy with which the cylindrical section of the tank had been honed, and now, moving under that magnificent sky, it looked like a marine animal of deadly beauty. A little further on, Daniel's motorbike made a change of direction and started to follow the truck. He thought he was lucky to have found it so casually, and a moment later he felt like laughing. Maybe following the tanker of a stranger was something absurd. The idea that the driver of that truck was the one who had delivered the package was just a guess. The only indication I had was that, when he left the bar after receiving the package, only that vehicle was missing that I remembered seeing parked there. It wasn't much; there might have been some other vehicle he didn't notice, or it might have been parked in the back. On the other hand, he was inside the bar for a good fifteen minutes and in that time, someone could have come in and made the delivery without him noticing.

Perhaps he had diverted his attention from the door too long when he deposited it on Camila. In any case, he had set out to get to the bottom of the matter and the only hypothesis he had was that Besides, something made him think that he hadn't missed the mark, as if an inner voice told him that he was right, that this guy was the one he was looking for, and he wasn't about to let the opportunity to get to the bottom of it slip away. He followed him at a safe distance, neither so great as to lose him nor so small as to alert him to his presence. He was aware that it could be hours before the truck stopped, but he was in no hurry; the tank of his Midnight was full and there was no one to wait for him at home.

About fifteen minutes after Daniel spotted his prey, the truck turned left, taking an unpaved road into the thicket. Daniel pressed the brake gently; he didn't want to be discovered. He followed him slowly, keeping his distance and cursing inwardly because he didn't like rolling his "girl" over bad tracks. The tanker drove on for another five or ten minutes along the path, and in its wake, there was a thick dusting which sometimes made it disappear from view. As it came out of a bend, it slowed down. The road widened a little and opened out on its left bank to form a wide clearing surrounded by undergrowth and trees. The truck moved into the woods and stopped, so that its right side was visible.

"I've got you," thought Daniel, and he also stopped his motorbike by pushing it off the road and hiding it in the bushes. He turned off the engine and got off quietly, approaching carefully into the clearing covered with foliage. A few yards before the road expanded, he seemed to find a perfect vantage point from which he could dominate most of the clearing without being seen. He crouched down and watched silently behind a bush. He heard the truck door open and someone get out. He could only see a pair of leather boots stuffed into worn—out jeans sticking out from under the truck, as the rest of the body was hidden by the truck. He felt his pulse racing. Soon he would see who this stranger was, although perhaps he was not as unknown as he thought. The thought made him uneasy. He saw how the boots were moving away and seemed to go into the trees. He hesitated for a second.

Should he follow him or wait for him to return? There didn't seem to be anything there, and the guy would have stopped to relieve his bladder. He thought it wise to wait and not be seen, he couldn't get away anyway.

About five minutes went by without anything happening. Daniel kept his eyes open, but the only noise he heard was the squawk of a bird or the lost chirp of a cicada. His legs started to get stiff from squatting and he ended up sitting on the floor to untangle them. To kill the wait, he took a cigarette out of the packet in his pocket, but when he went to get his lighter, he couldn't find it. His scowl was turned up in a nagging gesture. It was one of those old—fashioned metal benzine lighters, a Zippo with the chrome surface engraved. It was worn out by age and use, and he had had to change the wick and stone several times, but he was fond of it because it had belonged to his brother. His thoughts suddenly turned away from the lighter, however, because something else had claimed his attention. A scorpion that had emerged from a hole under a stone was slowly approaching where he was. His muscles tensed and he began to rise carefully. Although he did not believe his venom was lethal from the look of the animal, he had been stung by one of these bugs as a child and did not like the idea of repeating the experience. Without taking his eyes off the arthropod for a second, he carefully got up. Suddenly, he felt something hit his head and fell to the ground. His

[36

]

face was left on the ground and he thought his head was going to explode with pain, while he noticed that his vision was blurred. The last thing his eyes saw before he vanished was dusty black boots crushing the scorpion. In the background, the yellow silhouette of the tanker truck loomed up menacingly as its mind fused to black.

[37

]

CHAPTER 4

Daniel feels the cold kiss of the water through his neoprene suit while diving near the coast of Valparaíso. About ten meters up, the vague silhouette of the sun swaying from the surface looks like a bright planet from some distant galaxy. On that world, silence fills everything. Probably something similar must happen in outer space, thinks Daniel, as he slowly descends to allow his body to gradually adjust to the change in pressure. A little further down, he spots a tiny shoal of fish and heads towards them. He likes to see them turn away from him, forming a beautiful pattern with their shiny, elongated bodies, like a flock of starlings in the sky. He, too, feels like a fish. He notices the fins as the extension of his feet, which propel him downwards. Five more meters, ten, fifteen... In front of him an immense darkness opens, like an enormous black hole that shouts his name, that calls him with its foggy voice. And Daniel answers the call, leaving the blue surface waters to go into the dark green of the deep. His body feels free down there, just as the birds must feel, excused from obeying the force of gravity. As he continues to descend, he is entertained by the air expelled through his regulator, forming a multitude of glowing bubbles that play with his hasty ascent to the outside. He knows that it is not prudent to descend into those depths alone, that it should never, under any circumstances, be done, but he feels how the pelican pronounces his name and, like Ulysses before the song of the Sirens, he cannot resist the temptation to go to the invocation. He can hardly see more than two or three meters around him. The little light that reaches him from

[38

]

above and the particles suspended by the currents in the background greatly limit his visibility.

Suddenly he sees a huge stain that hovers enigmatic in front of him like a prehistoric animal. But instead of fear, he feels his chest swell with emotion. He knows exactly what it is, and he swims towards it. The figurehead of the sunken ship stands majestically as if welcoming him, and Daniel reaches out to touch its rusty surface covered with algae and molluscs. It truly looks like the skin of a dinosaur. It's shaped like a newt with half its tail missing. Admired, it caresses the rough surface of its forehead, the beards that intertwine on its chest and the conch that blows on its lips, from which a millenary sound seems to emerge. He dives a little further down and notices that the keel of the boat is buried in the sand and can hardly be distinguished from the sea bed. He goes around the port side, from which some corroded cannon appears, and a little further on, he can see a hole in the hull that opens up like a black mouth through which the fish enter and leave. He thinks that this is probably where death came to the ship, and he too enters through the hole, as if swallowed by a whale.

As he wanders through the throat of the ship in fascination, he imagines the last moments of the sailors who sailed through the waters in it without knowing that it would become their coffin. That forgotten ship in the stillness of the depths reminds Daniel of the smallness of human beings and the insignias of time. He has been there for centuries in patient custody, oblivious to what is happening to the world, like a silent watchman of the hidden secrets of the sea. Dazzled by his enormous skeleton, he dives among the wreckage and feels overwhelmed, as if he were in a sacred space, as if instead of being inside a sunken ship he was among the

[39
]

ruins of a phantasmagorical cathedral under the waters. A strange zenithal light unexpectedly bathes the scene, and Daniel, bewildered, looks up at the place from which it came. The beam of light filters through the remnants of what was once the roof, but what amazes him is not that, but a figure diving in its radiance, heading towards him. He is a young man whom he cannot make out well, but his figure is very familiar to him. Inexplicably, he is not wearing any diving equipment; no suit, no air tanks, no mask... When he is in front of him, he recognizes him immediately. He is Benjamin! His brother smiles at him and invites him to follow him. The two swims together through the wreckage of the boat, in waters that seem to have suddenly turned a splendid, luminous blue. Daniel feels as if he were bursting with joy swimming alongside his brother, chasing after each other, as when they were children and became entangled in the waves. He wants to ask him where he's been all these years, but underwater he can't do it, although that doesn't matter now either. Now they are together again and swimming happily among the fishes, under that supernatural light that seems to have given him back to him. I hardly remembered the features of his face, or his expression, but now that he is seeing him again, having him in front of him, the shadows that have covered his face all those years are fading away, and his smile is returning. From his neck hangs the small anchored cross his father gave him, which sways gently on its chain with the movement of the water. Daniel beckons his older brother to the surface, wants to see him outdoors in the sunlight to make sure it's not a dream. But Benjamin shakes his head and his brother notices that something is twisting in his gesture. He looks at him strangely and at that moment he realizes that his features are the same as they were twenty years ago, when he disappeared.

[40

]

Suddenly he feels a sharp pain on the back of his left hand. He holds it in his other hand while he notices that, a few meters behind his brother, a long shadow slips through the wreckage. He signals to Benjamin and him turns but sees nothing. Then, sensing danger, Daniel grabs his brother by the wrist and urges him again to follow him to the surface. Benjamin then looks regretfully at his younger brother and points out the black water behind him. Daniel turns and discovers that a whitish figure like a ghost wrapped in darkness is approaching them. When he realizes what which is, he loses his breath and lets out an inaudible scream that comes from his mouth wrapped in a bubble. Panic sets in as a four—meter squall encircles the two brothers in a deadly circle and begins to describe ever—narrowing orbits around them. The shark's very black eyes contrast with the whiteness of its jaws armed with several rows of sharp teeth. Daniel has no doubt that the animal is ready to attack at any moment and knows that a single one of its teeth can take off a leg in a matter of seconds. Then something even more amazing happens, which makes his blood run cold in his veins. The shark's skin gradually takes on a bright yellow hue, which eventually spreads throughout its anatomy. Benjamin then stands between the shark and his brother, and gestures at the shark to get away, to escape. Horrified, Daniel tries to pull Benjamin out of the shark's sight, but the pain in his hand comes back with an unheard—The sky stretched out before his eyes as if it were a huge blue winged butterfly flying towards immensity. The clouds, white as freshly washed, piled up on the horizon in puffy cumulus clouds, adopting curious shapes, which evolved with the whim of intensity. He is as if paralyzed and feels an invisible force pulling him, dragging him to the surface.

[41

]

Something seems to shake his limbs and he hears a voice in the distance calling him.

Daniel...

He stretches out his arms towards his brother and tries to rebel against what separates him from him, but he notices that he rises and moves away little by little without being able to do anything about it. He barely sees his brother and the yellow beast that surrounds him move. The strange force continues to pull him like a puppet master. He hears someone calling his name again.

He feels more and more confused as he approaches the surface, and the light that shines strongly on the water begins to dazzle him... He notices that something is trying to pull him away from the place where he is and hears the same voice calling him again.

Daniel...

He then realizes that he is carrying a package with him, a package that has come up with him from the dark depths of the abyss. Strange and assaulted by a bad feeling, he opens it moments before leaving that liquid universe to return to the outside from where it came. An indescribable horror takes hold of him when he discovers inside the package the torn off head of his brother who is watching him with an exorbitant but lifeless look. The waters around him slowly turn red, while a last impulse brings him to the surface, and he can finally scream. His eyes open and he stands up abruptly, panting, trying to find out where he is.

—You're finally back. —He hears the voice that had pronounced his name in the distance.

—What... who... —he stammers, as he tries to make out the blurred figure in front of him.

]

—What a strange place you've chosen to take a
nap!
Little by little the image comes into focus and he can
clearly perceive what the person talking to him looks like.
He is looking at him between worried and funny.
Daniel looks into her eyes and immediately recognizes
the fantastic opaline reflections around her pupils.

[43
]

CHAPTER 5

Daniel sat down on the floor and held his head in both hands. He felt the blood flow to his temples and each beat was like a hammer hitting them. His jacket and trousers were covered in dust and everything was spinning. He breathed in and leaned his neck back, rotating it gently, letting the air reach his face as he tried to position himself. The images slowly began to parade through his aching head, and he became aware of where he was and what had happened. The guy in the tanker truck...

—Shit...

—You don't have much of a wake—up call, do you? —He looked at Camila in confusion.

—Sorry," he excused himself... I wasn't after you...

—I hope so," replied Camila, smiling and holding out a bottle of water. What happened to you?

Daniel thanked her for the water and took a long drink that pleasantly refreshed his throat. He looked at the girl for a while in silence. Although he was in pain, he couldn't help but be seduced by that biker girl. Not only because of the beauty of her eyes, but also because of her personality. They had barely spoken and seemed to have found out more about him than some people he had been relating to for a long time. "I think you're a loner," he had told her. Looking at her now he found her to be an enigmatic woman; she too seemed to have something beneath the surface.

—Did you finally eat the cow? —he asked, returning the water bottle.

—Yes, it was very good! —Camila laughed heartily. If I'd known I'd find you, I'd have brought you a good steak.

—I think I could have done with it," he laughed.

What are you doing here?

—What do you think? I was looking for you, stranger," she replied with a mischievous smile.

—Well, you've found me," said Daniel, standing up and shaking the dust off his clothes. No, really...

—I have never been more serious," she said without losing her smile. It seemed to amuse her to keep the mystery going. It is you who have not answered my question.

—What question? —he said, going to where he had hidden his motorbike. Camila went after him. When Daniel saw his Midnight intact in the bushes, he breathed a sigh of relief.

—I asked you what had happened to you. Because something has happened to you, hasn't it? I don't think you were taking a nap...

This time it was he who smiled. He liked that girl. But I didn't think it was right to tell him the story now. After all, he didn't know her at all. Besides, it didn't make sense that she was just there by chance, on that road where not a single soul passed by. He decided to make up an excuse.

—I think I've been mugged. I stopped to... rest for a while. And I must have been hit with something, I don't really remember...

—Now...

Daniel realized from the girl's look that he had just offered the stupidest excuse in history.

—And they took a lot of stuff? —Mmm—hmm. —she asked in a tone that seemed to detect a certain irony.

—He said something disturbed as he felt his pockets.

"The box!", he suddenly thought. He rushed to the seat of his Yamaha and opened it, fearing that the man in the truck might have taken it. His fears were unfounded, it was there in the same place he had left it. In fact, if, as she suspected, this fellow had been the same man who had delivered the package, there was no point in his taking it away now. Although he was relieved that the box was still there, his image automatically brought back his restlessness and bad mood.

—Is the devil still locked up in there?

Daniel immediately closed the bag. He didn't want to talk to her about the box.

—But I think... He felt his pockets again, and as he did so he remembered that he had lost his brother's Zippo. That could be a good excuse to divert attention from the box. My lighter was stolen!

Camila narrowed her beautiful eyes and looked at it as if she were scanning it.

She gave the impression that she didn't believe a single word.

—Mmm... —And was it very expensive?

—Not really. But I was fond of him. He was one of those old—fashioned benzine Zippos. He had been with me for years," he said with heartfelt regret as he took a cigarette from his packet and put it in his mouth.
You won't have a light, right?

—A similar one to this? —asked Camila, as she pulled a metal lighter out of her jacket pocket, in which Daniel immediately recognized his Zippo.

—Really?! —he exclaimed incredulously. Where did you get it?

—I'm not lying. I told you I'd come looking for you, she said as she offered him a light. When you left, I stayed and talked to Clarita? You know... I eat you; I don't eat you...

—Daniel smiled as he lit his cigarette and took a deep breath. Fortunately, it seemed that the headache was starting to evaporate. After a while I noticed that something was shining on the floor. When I saw what it was, I got on the bike and went out in search of you.

—You were right that we would meet again.

—Yes, I'm very intuitive," she replied, gazing at the chrome surface of the lighter. "What does this letter mean? Any girlfriend?

—Jealous?

Right after I said that, Daniel regretted it.

What the hell was he thinking? He didn't know that girl at all. He saw her blush and didn't dislike it. Although he loved the ease with which Camila seemed to move through the world, he felt a certain pleasure in seeing her lose her self—confidence a little in that situation. In any case, he had to say something immediately to fix his blunder. The problem was that she couldn't think of anything.

—To tell you the truth, a little," replied Camila, quickly regaining her poise and looking at him with a challenging smile.

Then he was the one who was disturbed for a few moments.

—It's B for Benjamin, my brother," he said quickly to get himself out of trouble. Then he thought he should have said something about her comment instead. He had never been intimidated by girls before. What was wrong with him? He was behaving very clumsily. Was it the blow to the head? Or was it perhaps that particular girl?

—And this? —Camila pointed to a small cross that had been engraved next to her initials on the lighter.

—It's an anchored cross," said Daniel thoughtfully, taking the lighter from the girl's hands. It was her badge. A kind of symbol he liked to wear.

—Was it...?

—Well, Benjamin... —Died.

—I'm sorry,' she said, visibly upset. I shouldn't have asked...

Daniel realized the word he had just uttered. He died. It was the first time he'd verbalized it. That he assumed his brother was dead. A twinge of pain gripped his chest. He shouldn't have said that. She should have told the truth, that he had disappeared in an accident, that you really didn't know if he was alive or dead. As he elaborated those thoughts, he found the idea of his brother being alive more implausible, more ridiculous. In any case, he didn't feel like talking about it, explaining it.

—It's all right... —How did you find me? —he asked, putting his lighter in his pocket and trying not to let her see the uneasiness on his face. That girl seemed to have a sixth sense for reading faces.

—It wasn't easy, don't you think? I saw you leave in a westerly direction and took that same road. I asked around to everyone I could. The truth is that a bike like yours doesn't go unnoticed...

Daniel felt a tingle of pleasure when he heard those words. He was proud of his bike, and someone who praised his girl had already won half of it. That comment even made the shadows that had begun to form a moment ago in his mind dissolve. He definitely liked that biker girl.

—The hardest thing was to find you in this abandoned place.

What the hell have you lost around here? Lucky guy in the truck...

[48
]

All of Daniel's muscles contracted when he heard that.

—What truck?

A yellow tank.Salía de este mismo camino mientras yo circulaba por la carretera secundaria en la que desemboca.

—What did he look like?

—I don't know... —yellow, big...

—No, I mean... —the driver.

—I didn't really get a good look at him... —Brown, with a mustache... He was wearing sunglasses and a black jockey similar to basketball players, with a wide visor with text patterns... —Why?

"Pretty common traits," Daniel thought. Right away he couldn't think of anyone close to him who fit that description. But the truth is, It could be anyone.

—Curiosity," Daniel thought. I came across a truck and wanted to know if it was the same one?

—It wouldn't have anything to do with that guy who attacked you, would it? —No.

—she asked, probing him with her eyes.

"That woman was really smart," thought Daniel. Not only because she could read into people's souls, but because she seemed to be good at investigating and drawing conclusions. One only had to look at how she had managed to find him. If he wanted to keep his secret, he would have to be careful.

—I invite you to eat! —was the first thing he said to

CHAPTER 6

C gas station, decorated with native elements of amila and Daniel ate at the roadside bar of a Mapuche culture and crammed with shelves full of chocolates, magazines and countless other products, more or less useless, that are usually found in this type of establishment. The food was not bad, although it was a little greasy, and Daniel thought he could detect the taste of some other fried food cooked in the same oil as his steak. They could have chosen any other place, but Camila said she was hungry for wolf, and they went into the first place they found.

—No one would say you just devoured a cow," Daniel had joked as he watched Camila dispatch her empanada.

The conversation was very pleasant and, although they didn't go into the personal arena, the complicity that had been established between the two in their first meeting was immediately confirmed. They seemed to have many things in common; among them, a sense of humor. And also, according to Daniel's intuition, an internal conflict that was looming vaguely, a secret or an intimate sadness that neither of the two wanted to share with the other. But whatever Camila was hiding behind her beautiful eyes was not relevant at the time. They ate, laughed and toasted with beer. Time passed quickly and Daniel never thought about the mysterious package or the driver of the yellow truck again. He didn't even have a headache any more. It was as if that girl had the virtue of making the negative dissolve like an aspirin in a glass of water.

They were sitting next to a large window that opened onto the monotonous but beautiful landscape of the road, through which they could watch the coming and going of the vehicles as if on the panoramic screen of a cinema. As it could not be otherwise among bikers, the conversation soon turned to the world of two wheels. Both agreed that what they had with the road was more than just a hobby, that it was a very special relationship, almost like a drug, almost like sex.

—It happens to me like the song says," said Camila, "when the road turns, I let myself go.

Daniel felt fully identified with those words, and so he let the girl know.

—It should be our anthem," he proposed.

—Done! —she agreed.

He felt very good about that girl, but he wasn't sure what his feelings were for her. He had just met her, and it seemed they had been friends for a long time. In his life experience he knew that this kind of natural understanding could happen, although very rarely, so he was even glad that he went to that bar that morning to look for the damn package, because if he hadn't, he wouldn't have met her. As they became more intimate, he became more physically attracted to her. She wasn't a dazzling beauty, but she had a nice, well—proportioned body, swollen, well—formed breasts, and a neck that invited kissing. But, above all, her face opened those marine eyes, exotic and unfathomable as the ocean itself, which, like the sea, seemed to keep some secret in its depths. He would definitely like to kiss her. But he didn't know if he felt like starting a relationship with someone in those moments of his life. Actually, he thought, he didn't know if she was a match or not. That idea momentarily clouded his mood, but he put it off right away. He wanted to enjoy the company of his new friend and those moments, which, he realized, were the first he had felt really comfortable with in a long time. Specifically, since she received the first of the strange packages.

They talked and talked. Especially about motorcycles. When they had finished eating, they asked for a couple of machine coffees as a mere excuse to continue talking,

[51
]

and even Camila dared to smoke a cigarette. The conversation continued and both agreed that once the road catches up with you, it doesn't let you go anymore. They tried to describe to each other how they felt about motorcycles, what hooked them in that inexplicable but powerful way to that world, but sometimes they couldn't find the words.

It didn't matter, they both knew perfectly well what it was without saying. To feel the speed, to feel how the glands secrete adrenaline in your body just like benzine is injected into the cylinders of your bike, to fit perfectly into the road and let yourself go, as the song says... Let yourself go. Yeah, maybe that was the best way to define it. Something you couldn't do anywhere else, in your everyday life. The motorcycle meant adventure, freedom, meeting friends, speed. An infinite number of sensations that —both of them coincided— no one who was not a biker could understand. Anyone could enter the world of the motorcycle, as long as they could buy one, of course; but not everyone was seduced, not everyone was born for that. Only a chosen few let themselves be carried away, they abandoned themselves so much that they ended up being unavoidably caught. It was as if they belonged to a different race, to a type of non—conformist people who in some inexplicable way did not fit into the mould into which life had fitted them and needed to get out, to free themselves from that vital last to which others seemed to adapt perfectly. And the instrument of release was the motorbike. The members of that race, to which Camila and Daniel undoubtedly belonged, always ended up meeting and recognizing each other as equals. And invariably, the place where they ended up meeting was the same place where they had met: the road.

[52
]

—Many people tell me that a motorbike is a coffin with two

Why do I risk it," she said, playing with the curl of her finger on one of her hairs? They say I'm a madwoman, that I defy death...

—But you're not a crazy person, are you? —he asked, "and she was sensually entangling her hair.

—What do you think?

—Mmm... —He squinted, looking at her and pretending to be interesting. I'd say so.

She punched him in the shoulder with a little punch, frowning as a sulky little girl would.

—You'll be...!

—Hey! —Hey! —Daniel tried to defend himself, raising his palms in peace. You're not a dangerous madwoman, are you?

—Who knows," she challenged him with a mischievous look and smile, "so be careful.

—No, really," he said, "what do you say to those who ask you why you are risking your life?

She stopped smiling for a moment, bowed her head, and stared at him silently. It seemed to Daniel that he would like that moment, precisely that one among all the others, to stop as a photographic snapshot, in which he could see indefinitely how those two eyes contemplated him.

—I tell you, who the fuck wants to live forever?

Daniel couldn't help but laugh. Camila was right. Who the fuck would want to live without really feeling life, without it flowing intensely through their veins, every minute, every second, offering them the petrol that allows them to continue?

—I think what I like best about the bike is that it takes me out of this crazy fucking world and allows me to stay away from it," she suddenly said. Her voice had taken on a melancholy, barely perceptible hue. Yes, I have to go back sometime, but it's always me who decides when.

—It's the same for me," agreed Daniel. That feeling of being able to go wherever you want whenever you want...

—Exactly. Without having to explain yourself to anyone.

Then an idea crossed his mind, which at first seemed a little absurd, but he decided to put it on the table:

—Hey, why don't we go somewhere, run around on our motorbikes?

—When? —Now?

—Why not?

—And where would you like to go? —I don't know.

—I don't know... —Pucon?

—Just like that? That's a little over three hundred miles from where we are...

—Ah, I see you're giving up," he said, defying her with his eyes.

—I give up? —she was indignant.

—If you'd rather go back to that crazy fucking world...

—He sighed with a look of resignation.

—You know what? —she replied, raising her eyebrow in an expression which seemed to indicate that she was picking up the glove: Fuck that crazy fucking world!

CHAPTER 7

They rode all afternoon on their two motorcycles. Camila's was smaller, a Suzuki GS, but it seemed to have adapted to her like a glove and was sleek and fast. She rode along the road as if instead of rolling she was caressing the road, and it seemed to Daniel that the girl was completely transformed by riding her motorcycle, as if she were a Mapuche Indian riding her mount through the virgin lands of her ancestors. They decided to take turns at the head of the march, and they did so throughout the entire journey. The heat had gone down quite a bit and there was not much traffic, so the trip was very pleasant. For most of the route the mountains of the Andes Mountains accompanied them, majestic and distant, like silent watchmen observing their run from the east side of the road. The landscape was running in their wake like the frames of a fantastic film, and Daniel enjoyed it when he had Camila in front of him, seeing the elegance and precision with which she leaned to take the bends. He was wearing an aquamarine blue jacket with the Mapuche flag sewn on the back and his hair, which showed up under the helmet, was waving in the wind. Travelling with her made him relive the times when he was younger and did that kind of crazy stuff, when he had a whole world to explore and did not think twice about getting going. Halfway through, they passed a group of young bikers on smaller bikes, who greeted them with horns and raised hands. Daniel was pleased with the fraternal gesture of those biker puppies and was sure that Camila had made him smile too. In the restaurant, during the meal, she had told him that riding his motorbike was something as magical and special as

[56

]

playing an instrument, and now that he saw her in front of him, it seemed to him that, indeed, with every gesture, with every kilometer he rode, he was tearing the string of a guitar or pressing the keys of a piano. Somehow that was true, how could it not have occurred to him before? Every time you rode a motorbike you could hear the music of the road, and they were composing a beautiful melody together on the asphalt.

They arrived in Pucon when the sun's rays began to decline. They parked their bikes in the center of town and looked for a place to stay. It didn't take long for them to discover a charming little hostel. Its wooden façade and terracotta tile roof finished off by small attics reminded them of a small hotel that could be found in a Swiss spa town. Camila fell in love with the place immediately and decided to stay.

—Separated," she had hastened to answer when the manager asked if they wanted the room with a double bed.

Although she knew it was the right thing to do, since they hadn't talked about it and there was no reason in principle for two perfect strangers to share the bed, she felt a slight discomfort because of the girl's quick answer, although she didn't let her feelings go outside. He decided to reject that little bitter aftertaste that was trying to settle in his mind. In reality, it was not worthwhile for anything to spoil that day, which until then had been perfectly developed for him. Thinking about it, he realized that, in fact, it had not been like that. The day had started badly, with the receipt of the fourth package and the mysterious photos that someone had taken of him without his consent for years. Then it had got worse and worse with the hunt for the bloody yellow truck, and it had got even worse when the bloody one had knocked him out. But the strange thing about it all was that when he had thought of that day as "perfect", he had completely forgotten about those details. It's as if that trip through the central region of Chile, that melody that he and Camila had played together, had taken him away from all those events, which now seemed very distant to him. It was as if the motorcycles, the road and Camila were like a medicine that had gradually closed his wound, calming his pain little by little, until it practically disappeared. The yellow tanker, the box, the photographs... all that belonged to that "crazy fucking world" they had left behind. With that trip they had let themselves go, as their song said. And now they wouldn't let anything, or anyone spoil it for them.

They went up to the room to rest and cool off a bit from the trip, but it didn't take them ten minutes to be down again. Now it was Daniel who was hungry for wolf, although Camila wasn't far behind, so they decided to go in search of somewhere nearby to settle their stomachs. The last rays of the afternoon bathed the little streets of Pucón with a soft, almost unreal light, which gilded Camila's hair, and slipped down her forehead until it landed on her eyes, coloring them in completely different shades to those Daniel had seen up to that moment. He was constantly amazed by this disconcerting phenomenon and thought that, like the motorbike rolling along the road, Camila's irises seemed to be breaking down different musical notes as the quality of the light reaching them varied. A fresh breeze came in from the lake and delicately enveloped them, and Daniel inhaled hard to fill his lungs with the clean air of that place. Although he loved the smell of petrol and asphalt, he enjoyed nature, and let that pure atmosphere, slightly tinged by the smell of wood burning in some nearby kitchen, penetrate his bronchi slowly and oxygenate his body.

]

They had dinner in a pleasant place and laughed again and talked about motorcycles and anything else that landed in the conversation. It was as if they had a million things to tell each other, but in doing so they were careful not to go into too much intimate territory, as if they had both tacitly fixed a boundary that neither of them dared or wanted to cross. This did not prevent them from enjoying each other's company and a delicious dinner, much better than the greasy food in the roadhouse. At the end, ignoring the seven hundred kilometers that they had been carrying, they decided to go and continue the evening in a bar near Lake Villarrica.

—This place seems cool," said Daniel as he passed by a place where an old Dire Straits song was playing that seemed to invite them in.

They liked the interior of the bar and went to the back to look for a place to sit down. As they passed by the table where a group of boys were having a few drinks, one of them called them:

—Hey! —Weren't you the ones who passed us a few hours ago on the road?

—Maybe," answered Daniel amusingly, "we overtook a lot of people.

—Why do you think it was us? —I want to know, Camila.

—That jacket you're wearing," said the boy. "It's hard to forget!

Daniel and Camila laughed, and he recognized in them the group of bikers who had greeted them on the road with the horn. The boys invited them to sit with them, and although he might have liked a more intimate evening, he gladly accepted the invitation; it was always nice to have a chat with the new generation of bikers.

]

Camila also agreed, and they sat down with them. —
Dare they dare to have a Jägermeister with Red Bull?

—asked Maya, a stunning blonde who was already a
bit tipsy.

—I'd better get a beer," said Daniel, thinking about the
hangover the next day.

—Wow," commented Camila ironically, "now you're
the one who wants to go back to the 'crazy fucking
world'.

Daniel looked at her in surprise and started to laugh.
So, he was giving her back the challenge he had given
her in the morning. Well, if she had accepted it without
blinking and had travelled half the country with him, he
was not going to be less.

—I wanted to stay in the fucking sane world

—he joked, "but I don't wrinkle. You'll see I can outlast
you. Come on, those Jägermeister!

They all laughed and toasted when the bartender
brought the drinks. Daniel thought a kind of code had
been established between the two of them. There was a
black and white, boring, grey, monotonous world, which
was that "crazy fucking world". The world of everyday
life, of normal, grey people. A world to which one had to
return from time to time, because reality was like that
and it ended up imposing itself, and even that strange
special race that the bikers were, demanded their
tribute. Yes, it was a place where one had to return, but
where one did not have to stay long, so as not to lose
one's sanity. And then there was the world of the
motorcycle, which was a world of color, of adventure, of
freedom, of passion. The first one was really a world of
crazy people, because you really had to be crazy or blind
to do what most people did, stay locked up in the prisons
where society, their families or themselves had put them.
And instead of knocking those prisons down with a kick,

with fists until their knuckles were skinned, they reinforced them with their submission, with their silence, with their resignation, adding day after day, week after week, bricks of regret and misery to their empty lives. One Jägermeister led to another. The potent blend of liquor and energy drink renewed the strength of their somewhat exhausted bodies, and they were reinvigorated like the tanks on their motorcycles when they were refueled. The members of that group of boys were quite a bit younger than they were, none of them older than twenty—two or twenty—three. There were four girls and three boys. They had never been to Pucon and had gone there on vacation. Jacko, the biker who had recognized them, a strapping, good—looking guy who looked like the captain of a football team from a gringo movie and had somewhat crooked teeth, told them about a legend he had read in the travel guide.

—They say that the spirit of Tupaq, a Mapuche chief, lives at the bottom of the lake," he said, adding an air of mystery to each of his words. He hopes that one day Rucapillán, the volcano god, will return the woman who took him away as punishment for a disobedience. She is a Mapuche princess of amazing beauty, and the volcano wants her for him. Sometimes, she tries to escape... — In one gulp she emptied the rest of her Jägermeister, as if gathering strength to continue with her story, and then theatrically saved a small pause to better capture the attention of the audience. Daniel was amused at how he tried to adopt an enigmatic air, probably to impress the girls. When that happens," he continued, "Rucapillán gets angry and erupts. From the bottom of the lake, the Indian sees the expulsions from the angry mountain and knows that his beloved has been discovered again.

—It's a very sad legend," said Camila, "separated by a space as amazing as this one, and the two of them are buried without being able to see it, one under the waters and the other in the bowels of the rock. What's her name?

—Ailin," said Jacko, satisfied with the interest in his story.

—Ailin," repeated Camila with a hint of sadness in her voice.

Daniel was captivated by the changing personality of his travelling companion. At one moment she was the brave and wild biker girl, and the next moment she was a sensitive girl with a melancholic look. In a way, she reminded him a little of himself.

—But that's not the end of the story," Jacko continued, adding a slightly dark tone to his voice.

—Yes? Tell! Tell! —begged Vera, a freckled redhead who listened to the story full of emotion. The alcohol circulating in the bodies of those present helped to make the story more and more intriguing.

—The years under the surface of the lake's waters have upset the Mapuche Indian, and they say that on nights with a full moon it is better not to bathe in the lake, because... Tupaq comes to take revenge on the volcano by claiming a victim...

—That Tupaq is crazy! —Rio Maya with a vengeance.

They continued talking for a while until the bar closed, and then Vera suggested buying a bottle of Jägermeister and some Red Bulls to go drink at the lakeside.

—Luckily, we see Tupaq! —Camila joked.

The possibility of seeing the Mapuche was not so far—fetched, as that night a very white moon, as round as a cheese, was hanging from the clear sky of Pucón. The lake spread imposingly before their eyes and, seduced by the magic of the moment, the kids bordered a stretch of its shore until they reached the northern flank, on a remote shore surrounded by conifers, from where they could have a good perspective of the volcano. The mountain rose majestically before them and its disturbing beauty was reflected in the waters of the lake, as a fearsome warning to the unfortunate Tupaq. Above the volcano, the full moon cast its light on the surface of the waters, filling them with infinite silver reflections.

—Let's go for a swim! —proposed Jacko, taking off his shirt awkwardly. The alcohol hindered his movements, but it made him want to have some fun.

—What if we disturb Tupaq? —Rio Maya, imitating the boy and taking off his clothes as well.

—Fuck Tupaq! —shouted Jacko, as he ran in his underwear into the water.

Camila looked at Daniel, and he answered with a knowing smile. Without thinking twice, they both stayed in their underwear too, and after a few moments the group of friends swam under the stars in the warm waters of the lake. Daniel picked up Camila in his arms and threw her forward, and she shouted in amusement as she dived in with the impulse, splashing the others. The water temperature was magnificent, and a gentle breeze descended from the side of the volcano caressing their wet bodies. Daniel watched Camila move freely in the water and was excited to see the drops fall on her naked, moonlit breasts. Then he suddenly felt the pain on the back of his hand again. The damned spider's bite did not seem to have healed at all.

—What have you got there? —asked Camila, reaching out to him.

—It's nothing," said Daniel, pulling his hair that had slipped off his face.

[63
]

—I looked at it while we were eating this morning. It doesn't look very good.

—You, on the other hand, did provoke it.

She bent her face flirtatiously and stared at him without saying anything. The pale night light transformed the iris of her eyes again, giving them a lunar hue. Behind her, the huge volcano seemed to encourage Daniel to take another step.

—If you stay here long enough, I think Rucapillán will let the princess go and catch you," he dared to say, interpreting her silence as an invitation.

Daniel had the impression that his words were having the opposite effect on Camila's mood to the one they were looking for, because the joy on her face seemed to be transformed into a sudden sadness, similar to the one she showed in the bar when she heard the story of Tupaq and his princess.

—A bit corny? —asked Daniel, a little troubled.

She kept silent for a few moments. Then he answered distantly:

—Yes, very much so.

Daniel took her by the hand and stared at her.

—I..." she said in a trembling voice, looking away. "You must know that... I will never kiss you...

Daniel was stumped. What did that mean? He turned away from her slightly, as if he needed some space to understand, but he didn't stop looking at her, confused, like an idiot, not knowing what to do or what to say. He didn't understand anything. He hadn't asked her for a kiss. But, above all, he didn't understand how those absurd words could have hurt her so much. I didn't know this girl at all. And he seemed to know her less and less. She looked at him again and when she realized the effect that what she had just said had had, her gaze changed again, although the sadness remained in her. Then, as if she herself did not know what she was doing, as if a spring moved her involuntarily, she brought her lips closer to his and placed them minimally on them, as if she were afraid of being rejected. Daniel felt himself tremble at her touch, like a teenager at the first kiss. But he was not a teenager, he was an adult, and he allowed his tongue to enter her mouth and discover its taste. She, denying the words he had just uttered, let herself be invaded by his tongue and enjoyed its journey, while he joined her body to the biker's, letting himself go, just as the song said. Daniel noticed how his body responded to her contact, hardening under the water, and he took her in his arms, drawing her against him. Then he held her by the back of her neck and gently caressed her back as he continued to kiss her, losing track of where he was, letting the girl's incomprehensible words fade away into the past, emptying his mind of any other thoughts, entangling his consciousness in the back of the biker's machine, in her breasts, in her mouth, as if his hands and lips needed to release

The two of them are able to concentrate on everything else, as if they needed to concentrate all their senses on the act of riding their body, just as they did when they rode their motorbike on the road.

But in a few moments, it all turned into madness. They heard a deafening roar that left them paralyzed. It was the roar of the mountain, as if the Mapuche princess had tried to escape once again, enraging Ruca—Piptan. Everyone turned their gaze to the sizzling sound coming from the god's mouth, which in a few seconds lit up the night sky with a brilliant reddish orange. Like a bad omen, the moon seemed to be stained with blood, and Camila held Daniel tightly in her arms, overwhelmed by the sight of the column of lava rising like a glowing tongue that wanted to lick the sky. The mountain top sparkled with the eruption and a vast mass of smoke and ashes rose like a colossal mantle covering the stars until they disappeared in the shadows.

—It is the Mapuche Gods..." Camila said, turning away from him as if hypnotized by the fury of nature. "They are the Gods who seek revenge...

—What do you mean? —he asked in surprise.

—It's the wound... The volcano bleeds from the crater its pain... and its rage...

Daniel didn't understand those words, but he drew her to him and embraced her. She rested her face on his shoulder and let herself be protected in shock. The biker raised his eyes to the furious flames Rucapillán was spitting out of his mouth, and he couldn't help but shudder at the thought of the words Camila had just uttered.

They are the gods who seek revenge.

CHAPTER 8

eyes. He wasn't quite sure where he was and t would be around noon when Daniel opened his lazily rubbed his sleepy eyelids. He was lying on the right side of his body and in front of him was a pale green wooden cupboard with the paint somewhat peeling, which he didn't recognize. He felt a twinge in his head, as if tiny beings were sticking pins in it. There were hazy images from last night that came to him in bursts. It was not clear to him whether the pain was due to the blow he had received the day before or to Jägermeister's hangover from Red Bull. Actually, he had been a little reckless, he thought. He had been unconscious for quite a while because of the attack by the guy in the yellow truck and hadn't even been to the hospital. The most reasonable thing to do would have been to have X—rays taken and to have been kept under observation for a while. But he let himself go for the moment. The food, the conversation, the trip—everything had come up very spontaneously, almost without thinking. He was so comfortable with Camila and felt so close to her when they talked about motorcycles that he could not help but propose that she go on an adventure. In that he was very much like his brother, in the unthinking way he took life, of living it simply as it came, almost in bites, as if it were going to end at any moment, as if everything you didn't eat from the cake that existence offered you was an insult to heaven itself. One of Benjamin's favorite phrases came to mind and he couldn't help but smile.

"To live is a verb that is only conjugated in one tense: now." Like so many other things his brother had taught him, and he had put in his existential rucksack, he had

[68
]

also appropriated that phrase. But Benjamin was no longer there, he had pushed life to the limit and had taken all the pieces of cake he could, but with one of them, the last one, he was attracted. Daniel painfully remembered that a few hours earlier he had told Camila that her brother had died, and in those moments, he perceived those words as a betrayal. He felt another prick on his head; those damned dwarves were working their way through his skull. He noticed the doughy mouth and the dry throat. That was definitely the hangover. He knew he should have listened to his experience and kept on drinking beer. But he and Camila loved getting drunk, and he wasn't willing to fall behind if she challenged him. He was surprised to realize that he was thinking of her as someone he had known all along, even though he had not even heard of her existence for a couple of days. He looked at the green cupboard strangely again and wondered once more where it was. Next to it was a coat rack from which Camila's jacket hung. He stared at its somewhat worn—out surface, especially at the elbows, and at the original color that highlighted the Mapuche flag inscribed in the center. He thought about what that big guy from the motorcycle group had said, what was his name again? Jacko. Kind of hard to forget a garment like that. He was right. He felt that the headache had subsided a bit and slowly turned his body, trying not to attract the attention of the sadistic little men who were torturing his brains. As he turned around, he saw her there, five feet away from him, in another bed. Now he was beginning to remember. That wasn't the room at Pucon's hostel. The eruption of the volcano had been spectacular but short, and the local authorities, although they had raised the alert level, had not considered it necessary to evacuate the population from the city. Nevertheless, he and Camila had decided as a precaution to move to Villarrica, which was a little further away. There they found that cheap and somewhat dreary hostel, but more than enough for what they needed: sleep. Daniel observed how the morning light filtered through the half—opened blinds. It formed thin golden beams in which tiny particles of dust floated that looked like stars suspended in a distant galaxy to him.

The sun poured gently on Camila's body, which slept unaware that Daniel was watching her. Little specks of sunlight rested on her face, as if the day wanted to kiss her. Daniel sat up on the bed trying not to make any noise and stayed there, in his underwear, looking at her. The headache was compounded by the discomfort he felt at the sight of the sleeping girl. In fact, he had never seen her as beautiful as she was now, with the sun flecking her face, but that beauty was also painful, because it seemed to be forbidden to him. That adventure was supposed to be a beautiful thing, and indeed it was, but there was something that didn't fit, that made him think that that wonderful piece of cake, the sweetest he had tasted in a long time, wasn't for him. He tried to remember Camila's words the night before. He said something like he would never kiss her. That was illogical, because she then kissed him. But after that kiss and those that followed it was hard for him to consider the possibility that he might not be able to kiss those lips again. He kept looking at her for a long time, imagining the color of her eyes when she woke up. Her hair was fluttering on her pillow and a lock of hair crossed her cheek like a small stream that flowed into her mouth. She thought of pushing it away, but preferred not to touch it, she didn't want it to wake up. He was hungry and also wanted to take an aspirin, but he remained still, as still as a predator on the savannah keeps watch over its prey, without moving a single muscle so as not to alert

[70
]

it. Any noise, any small change in the room, could disrupt that magical moment. He did not want it to wake up, he wanted to be able to contemplate it like that for hours, because at that moment it was his; only his image, yes, but he had it there, only for him. Something made him feel — perhaps his words the night before, or the shock of the volcano's eruption — that he would never see her again. He felt his chest shrink with that thought and tried to push it away. It was absurd. Why should he not see her again?

They had become good friends, or at least they liked each other very much. They had so much in common. The bikes, the road. They were part of her life, they were members of that special breed, the bikers. Then he remembered that they even had a song of their own. A cloud must have crossed with the sun, because the beams of light suddenly disappeared and with them the specks that dotted Camila's face. Daniel looked at her body. She was lying face down and through the sheet the path of her anatomy was hinted at, a smooth and winding orography like the road that led them there, a road of skin that he would like to travel now with his mouth. He felt an incipient erection begin to take shape under his underpants. He looked back at his face. Letting go... That's what he was doing, letting go. But he had to stop that. It didn't make sense for him to have such thoughts of loss. He barely knew this girl and he couldn't be in love with her. He just liked her a lot, that's all. But he was free, and he didn't want to feel tied to anything or anyone. The only thing he felt tied to be the Midnight Star, but that was only because his girl was able to cut all the other strings, to break with her vibrating engine all the ties that held Daniel to the ground and let him fly.

[71
]

Suddenly, Camila opened her eyes. The radiant color they showed when they woke up accelerated Daniel's pulse. She smiled at him, and said in a drowsy voice

—Mmm... —Good morning.

Then the girl's gaze shifted to Daniel's underpants, where the physiological effects caused by the contemplation of his sleeping body still remained. He noticed, got up quickly and turned around, heading for the chair where his clothes were. He felt his face burn with blush, but fortunately, being on his back, she couldn't see him.

—How... how did you sleep? he said half—heartedly as he put on his trousers.

—Well, thank you... —You seem to be on your way, don't you? — she replied as she stretched out her arms. In her tone of voice Daniel seemed to detect a mocking note.

—Yes," he replied, ignoring the hint, in case it was one, as he had just fastened his trousers. I'm so hungry I'm dying.

—Me too," she agreed, before giving a huge yawn.

—Welcome to the club!

Fifteen minutes later they were having breakfast in a bar near the hostel. The aroma of freshly brewed coffee from the steaming cups reawakened their senses, still a little lethargic from recent sleep and hangovers. They were sitting by a window, similar to the one they sat by to eat at the roadhouse bar, but from there they had a very different perspective. In the distance they could see the volcanic massif, from whose crater a slight white plume emerged, a vestige of their fury from the day before. The cone of Ruca— pillán stood solemnly and defiantly in the sky like a silent threat.

[72

]

—Half the scare of yesterday, eh? —said Daniel, dissolving an effervescent aspirin in a glass of water.

—Yes," said Camila, looking at the contents of her coffee cup, as if the memory weighed heavily on her.

Daniel looked at the bubbling of the aspirin as he left, falling into the water and the foam that was forming on the surface brought the rash to his head.

—I hope this will take away my headache," he said, and drank the contents of the glass in one gulp.

—Are you going to tell me how you got that wound in the end?

—she asked as she saw the erosion on the skin of her hand, which had become evident as she lifted the glass to drink.

Daniel thought they looked more alike than they wanted to remember. She, for some reason she couldn't imagine, didn't feel like talking about the volcano episode. And he didn't want to talk to her about that wound either. That made him think of the packages, the pictures, and the guy in the truck. It was the first time he thought about it since he had woken up. In fact, since they arrived in Pucón he had hardly remembered it. It was strange for him to realize that. The day before he had found out that someone close to him had been photographing him over the years without his consent, and something that had meant such a radical turn in what he had thought was his life until then seemed to have been momentarily erased from his memory. Maybe it was that strange and magical place, with the lake, with the volcano, with the fantastic legend of the Mapuche chief Tupaq and Princess Ailin... Or maybe it was her.

—Well? —Maybe it was her. —insisted Camila with an impatient look on her face.

voice.

[73

]

—It's nothing, just a scratch," he said, glancing absently at the television in the bar. They were broadcasting the news, and, on the screen, there were some spectacular images of the volcano in eruption that some private person had taken with his cell phone. —Does it have anything to do with yesterday's attack? —asked Camila.

He turned to her and stared at her. That girl was very intuitive. But he could also, if he wanted to, ask her a few questions. What did she mean by not kissing him? Why did she talk about the revenge of the gods? What was the reason for the sadness that lay behind those beautiful eyes? However, I would not question her. I had a feeling she would not like it, and I did not want to spoil the end of the journey. Besides, if she had something to tell him, he preferred her to do it freely, because he had decided to do so.

—Okay... —You don't have to tell me if you don't want —she said, looking thoughtfully at the window.

—It's a long story," he replied.

And without knowing how or why, he found himself explaining to Camila about the four packages and their strange contents. He told her about the huge spider that had bitten him, about the chicken with its throat cut and about the insect mess, but for the moment something made him not mention the photographs. He also told her about his suspicions about the driver of the tanker, and how he followed him when he found him by chance on the road. She listened attentively, silently, as if trying to digest that disconcerting story.

—Are you sure there were four packages? —she asked when he had finished speaking.

—Yes, why? —he replied, offering her tobacco.

—No reason,' she said, refusing the offer and then looking at him silently as if meditating on what he had just said.

Daniel did light a cigarette. He left the pack and the lighter on the table and took a deep breath. The aspirin had done its job effectively and with surprising speed, and the little men in his head were struggling in retreat. He felt that a weight had been lifted off his shoulders by telling Camila about it, even if he had left a small part of it in the inkwell. Relaxed and happy he stretched his legs and looked up at the top of the volcano.

—Look! —he said suddenly. He lifted his jaw and formed a U shape with his lips, through which he exhaled rings of smoke which slowly expanded as they rose towards the roof. I am Rucapillán!

She barely smiled. She took the Zippo from the table and looked thoughtfully at the letter and cross inscribed on its shiny metal surface, bathed in the light that streamed through the window.

—You said there were four packs,' she said as if hypnotized, 'and they were made by the reverberations of the sun on the lighter.

What was in the room?

—You can't keep anything from yourself, can you? — he snorted and looked at her with a smile.

She gave it back to him and waited attentively for the answer. Daniel gave up. He didn't feel like telling anyone about the photos. He didn't even feel like thinking about it. But at some point, he would have to tell someone, and who better than someone outside his circle of friends. For all I knew, any one of them could have been the one who took the pictures. So, he told them. He explained his amazement at finding them in the box and the nakedness he had experienced. He also told her that he had gone to that bar hoping that in that last package he would find the answer to that mystery and be able to talk to the person who had sent them.

—The rest you know," he concluded.

—Who could have done that? —said Camila thoughtfully, turning the Zippo in her hand. And for what?

—That's the million— The sky stretched out before his eyes as if it were a huge blue—winged butterfly flying towards immensity. The clouds, white as freshly washed, piled up on the horizon in puffy cumulus clouds, adopting curious shapes, which evolved with the whim dollar question! —He tried to joke and ease the matter in front of the girl, although it was clear to her face that it was a matter of great concern.

—Well, we'll have to ask someone.

—Will we? —he looked at her in surprise.

—You don't think I'm going to be left wanting to solve this mystery, do you? —she replied with a mischievous smile.

That smile gave Daniel some comfort. Telling the story had spoiled his good mood, and Camila's seriousness and silence had done little to improve it. The girl's eyes were changing again in the changing light of the day and he thought he could never get tired of contemplating those transformations. Then he came up with a funny idea. Maybe that color changed with thoughts or emotions. Maybe every emotion had a special color. Someone who could study those changes and associate them with their corresponding emotions could discover the secrets that Camila held in her heart.

—What are you thinking about? —she asked.

—Guess.

Camila looked at him carefully, as if she really wanted to guess the thought, and Daniel had the feeling again

]

that she was scanning him, as when he lied to her about being mugged. Although it was absurd, it made him feel uncomfortable.

Suddenly Camila's gaze seemed to be absorbed in a point that was beyond Daniel.

—I thought it might be fun if you and I played detective together," said this one, claiming his interest.

Sherlock Daniel and Camila Watson!

Camila didn't answer, she didn't even seem to have heard Daniel's words. Her attention was elsewhere, and her eyes expressed a mixture of astonishment and concern. He followed her gaze to the television screen, where he could see the image of a white sheet apparently covering a dead body on the street pavement. A safety zone around the body was cordoned off with yellow tape, and on the other side a group of curious people were crowded together, illuminated by the flashing lights of a police vehicle. The camera lens left the body and swept vertically along the facade of the adjacent building until it zoomed in on the roof. A voiceover was reporting:

...and this is the third case in the last few hours. The pattern appears to be the same as in the first two, but the CID investigators interviewed by us have not confirmed this and prefer to keep the information to themselves so as not to jeopardise the investigation. As you will recall, both the first suicide bomber and the second had received five packages from an unknown sender whose contents have not been disclosed. According to eyewitnesses, in both cases, the receipt of the fifth package was the trigger that drove the victims to throw themselves off the buildings. In this case, the building chosen was the well—known Marriott Hotel, located on President Kennedy Avenue in the capital. A peculiarity on which a line of police investigation has been opened is the presence of a strange mask that the first two suicides wore when they threw themselves into the void. According to official sources, both masks were made of wood and represented a bird. The authorities are considering the possibility of some kind of macabre ritual...

Daniel was petrified to hear that information. Some people had received a few miscellaneous packages and ended up dead. Would the person who sent those packages be the same person who sent him his? And in that case, was he in danger? The headache came suddenly again, and a general malaise came over him. He was confused. What the hell did those packages mean and what did they have to do with him? He turned to Camila and found hers full of concern.

—If... if you have received four packages and the one who sent them is the same as the one who sent the packages of those people, then..." she began to say in a barely audible voice.

Daniel finished the sentence:

—Then there's only one more left.

]

CHAPTER 9

They left Villarrica the sun had been swirling the temperature had dropped a little and since around the clouds, hiding its rays and offering the bikers a truce on their return journey. Daniel felt alive again, the headache had completely disappeared, and the air was licking his face as he gained miles on the asphalt. His Midnight and the road possessed a kind of healing power that made him recover both physically and mentally like nothing else he had ever known. The noise of the engine, the continual rumble of his wind—shaken jacket, the vibration of the handlebars — each and every one of those familiar sensations made him feel renewed. He looked in the rearview mirror and saw Camila leaning elegantly over her Suzuki, like an Amazon riding her saddle. He breathed in the smell of the road, the smell of wet grass mixed with the smell of gasoline and the smoke of combustion and felt it as a gift. She was home again. Greyish clouds swirled before him, and seemed to engulf the road a few miles ahead, and he feared that they would be surprised by the rain. On both sides of the road, on oceans of greenery, the power lines stretched between the posts like staves of a large score on which to write the notes of the tune they were playing as they rode their motorcycles — the music of the road. He noticed a handful of cows on his right that were grazing quietly in a small meadow and waved them to Camila. Through the mirror, he saw her gesture back with her thumb up and imagined her smile behind the visor. He also smiled as he saw that many of them were looking north. They rolled around for another half hour when, as he had feared, a drop of water fell on his ungloved hand.

[

A sign on which the raindrops began to chime gave the location of a rest area ten kilometers away. Daniel looked up at the increasingly leaden sky and pointed at the sign, indicating that they could stop there. They had already travelled quite a long way and could do with a rest. Besides, the first drops of rain on the mud and the mud deposited on the pavement could be a risk factor, so it was advisable to make a stop. They drove through the rain on the stretch of road that separated them from the area, and by the time they arrived, the sky began to pour down so hard that you could hardly see it from a few meters away.

—Phew, that was close! —exclaimed Camila as they stood the motorcycles under a canopy next to the establishment.

—We've left the good old days behind us," he said, opening the door to the shop.

—It doesn't matter," she said in a good mood as she entered, "there's no harm in it, I was already hungry.

Once again, they found room by the window, although this time their gaze could hardly penetrate the thick watery mantle that stood between them and the landscape. As they brought them some sandwiches, Camila was mesmerized by the random route of the drops that had splashed on the window, while she fiddled mechanically with a bottle of ketchup on the table. Daniel watched her, amused; he loved to see her so absorbed in the whimsical trajectories that the drops formed as they descended through the glass. Her wet hair had curled up a little, giving her face a more youthful appearance, which was reflected in the glass surface, doubling its beauty. Thunder rumbled outside as if a battalion of giants were pounding furiously at the clouds.

—We have to rule out possible suspects," she said suddenly without looking away from the glass.

[

—So that little head is still working at full speed, even though it seems to be in the clouds! —laughed Daniel as he listened to the girl's words.

—Seriously, Daniel, you don't have much time," Camila replied gravely, looking back at him. Is there anyone who has keys to your house?

—You mean because of the photos?

—Yes.

Daniel thought for a moment about the answer while he took a cigarette out of the packet and lit it.

—I don't know...; we're talking about quite a few years, —he said meditating as he let out the smoke on the table. My mother used to have it, but it's not there anymore... Also, Hector, my best friend. Maybe my sister. And Mapuca, of course.

—Who's Mapuca? —I want to know Camila.

—She's like a second mother to me, —he replied with a tender gleam in his eye. —She came to work at home when I was little and has always been there. He asked me for the keys when I moved into the apartment to come clean.

—You love her very much, don't you?

—Yes. —I'm sure she hasn't been, it wouldn't make any sense.

—And the others?

—The truth is, neither did she. My sister, Hector... They interrupted the conversation when the waiter came to serve them the sandwiches and some refreshments. Camila voraciously threw herself into devouring theirs, after loading it with mustard and ketchup. Daniel preferred to finish his cigarette before starting, while he entertained himself by looking at a newspaper on the table.

[

—My ex, Andrea, also had keys," he remembered, "but he gave them back to me when we finished.

Camila's face twisted almost imperceptibly at those words, but she just nodded her head and continued to eat. However, that little disturbance did not go unnoticed by Daniel, who smiled to himself. He poured his Coke into the glass and a brown foam formed on the surface of the drink.

—How long ago did you leave it? —she asked absently, looking at the window. The rain was coming down outside in the dark, I was just getting into the evening as if it were already dark.

—A couple of years,' he said, 'but it wasn't her, there are pictures taken later.

—The keys can be copied before they are returned, you know? —grunted Camila as she chewed her sandwich.

—Jealous? —he asked amusingly.

—This is no laughing matter, Daniel," she replied angrily, and left the rest of the sandwich on the plate, as if she had lost her appetite.

—It was just a joke," he began to say, "the other time I told you...

—Listen," she interrupted. "You and I have nothing, and we're not going to have it.

—It didn't seem that way on the night of the lake," he answered, confused and upset by the girl's change of attitude.

—I'm sorry," she said, as if regretting her words. Please, forget it. Let's talk about the pictures.

A flash of lightning flashed outside and lit up the sky behind the glass. Daniel crushed his grumpy cigarette into an ashtray in which several unlit cigarette butts lay.

—I don't think it was her," he said, taking his sandwich and seasoning the sausage inside with a little mustard. The first pictures were taken when we weren't going out yet.

—I don't know..." said Camila thoughtfully. "What other people do you have around you?

Tell me about your work, your friends...

—Do you think I haven't thought about all that already? —he replied, taking a bite of his sandwich.

—You're angry... —she said sullenly.

—No, really, it's all right. —Daniel didn't want to spoil his day, so he offered to give her the information she asked for. My family owns a conglomerate company with four other partners. When my mother died, they offered me the address, but I refused. I wasn't interested in the business; I would have felt trapped there, dressed like a penguin, all day with meetings and shit like that...

Camila smiled when she heard that, and her smile somewhat dissipated the tension that had settled between the two.

—What? —he asked, smiling in return.

—I can't imagine you in a suit, with a shirt and tie.

Daniel laughed when he heard that, and some breadcrumbs came out of his mouth with laughter. Camila took a paper napkin from a dispenser and wiped some mustard off the corners of his mouth.

—Well, it doesn't look so bad," he boasted, "I've had to take it sometime. But yes, you are right. I am much more comfortable in my leather jacket.

—Of that I have no doubt," laughed Camila, and took the newspaper to leaf through it while Daniel was counting his sandwich.

So, you're a rich kid? —he added.

[

—You could say that," admitted Daniel with a bored look on his face.

—Maybe that has something to do with the packages...

—What could it possibly have to do with? —he asked. There's nothing unusual in the photos... I don't think they want to blackmail me. Besides, I'm disassociated from the family business.

Camila looked at him for a long time. Her opaline eyes reflected a strange sadness. Out of the blue, she reached out and took his hand.

—I don't want you to jump out of the window," she exclaimed.

Daniel, a little perplexed by this gesture, smiled and squeezed her hand.

—I have no intention of doing that," he said with a smile, "and if I do, I'll choose the mask myself," he joked. I'm not going to wear the mask of one of those birds.

Camila's eyes got wet and she looked down. Daniel took her chin delicately in his hand and raised it so that he could look at her.

—Hey, I'm not going to kill myself," he said softly. I have no reason to do that.

She looked back at the newspaper and continued to leaf through it in silence. Outside the storm seemed to be easing and the thunder was coming farther and farther away.

—My mother says that thunder is the voice from heaven that scolds men when they have done something wrong," she said without looking away from the paper.

—I'm sure she's very pretty if she looks like you," he said.

[

—She is," she replied with a hint of sadness in her voice.

—Is something wrong? —asked Daniel.

—No, nothing's wrong.

—That makes me think you've asked me a lot of questions, but I hardly know anything about you.

—My life is not interesting," she said, turning the page of the newspaper.

Suddenly, Daniel's gaze was fixed on the page that had just come into view. His heart began to beat strongly, and he snatched the newspaper from Camila to get a better look at it.

—Hey, you only had to ask for it! —she exclaimed annoyed.

—Look! —he pointed out, very upset, the photograph of a logo that appeared in one of the newspaper advertisements.

She turned him over and looked at him. It was a commercial sign with a company name on a black figure schematically representing a shark. Below it was the company's address and a telephone number.

—Jaws Transport? —he asked strangely.

—The company logo! —He said. It was printed on the tanker! Camila opened her eyes in surprise.

—We got it! —she exclaimed, hurrying to look for her cell phone in her jacket pocket. We're going to call!

—Just a moment! —He stopped her. Let's investigate a bit first...

She nodded her head and googled the name of the company. The search yielded many results, but Camila entered the link that led to what looked like the official site, because the name of the URL was the same as the firm's name.

—It is a transport company that operates all over

[

Chile
—she explained as she read the information offered by the website. It belongs to a major corporation called Bildex. The head office is located...
—Wait! —Daniel interrupted her, taking the cell phone in his hand and looking avidly at the screen. Did you say Bildex?
—You definitely don't feel the need to ask for things today, she reproached him with annoyance at his abruptness. Yes, you know that company?
—It belongs to Hugo Areilza, one of the four partners in our family business.

CHAPTER 10

T he next morning, they were both in front of the Titanium Tower, a vast elliptical —based skyscraper located on Andres Bello Avenue in the Chilean capital. The glass surface reflected like a mirror the nearby buildings and the sky of Santiago full of white clouds. On the fifty—first floor was the headquarters of Bildex S. A., the company whose majority shareholder was Hugo Areilza.

They had traveled all afternoon the day before on their motorcycles and arrived in Santiago when it began to get dark. They decided to go to rest and met at eleven o'clock in Bildex to interview Areilza. Daniel assured Camila that he knew him very well; he had been a friend and partner of his parents and would receive him without any problem. Both were willing to get to the bottom of the matter.

The secretary kindly greeted Daniel, whom she knew from other occasions. While he was talking to her, he absentmindedly rummaged through the pamphlets that lay in a methacrylate display on the reception desk, picked one up, and put it away. The secretary moved them to an adjoining room where no one else was waiting.

—Tremendous half water! —exclaimed Camila with astonishment when they were left alone.

The room they were in was decorated in a minimalist and modern but luxurious way. On the hardwood walls hung some abstract paintings in strategic positions, the floor was carpeted in shades of sand to match the furniture, and a magnificent pyramid lamp hung from the ceiling. The girl approached the gigantic window that

[

followed the oval shape of the façade and contemplated the city at her feet, under the snowy peaks of the Andes.

—Is your apartment like that too? —she asked Daniel, fascinated by the spectacular view of the city from that height.

—He replied, trying to eliminate any trace of presumption in his voice.

—You must be loaded! —she laughed, not taking her eyes off the splendid view before her.

He looked at her silhouette as a biker cut out against the city and tried to imagine what she would look like in a tight dress and high heels.

—Well, what an honor! —said a female voice behind him which made them both turn around.

A very beautiful girl, about thirty years old, dressed in an elegant, tight dress, whose very short skirt was tangled up in her long, well—turned legs, had entered the room and was walking towards Daniel with a big smile on her lips.

—Andrea! —exclaimed he, when he recognized her, stretching out his arms to greet her.

—What good does it do you here? —she said, hugging him and giving him a kiss on the mouth in a way that Camila found too conspicuous.

—Camila, this is Andrea," said Daniel, visibly uncomfortable at Andrea's gesture.

—I'm delighted," he said, approaching Camila and giving her a kiss on each cheek, then turning to Daniel, he added with a smile: "You still have great taste in girls, lover boy!

—We're just friends," said Camila, somewhat annoyed at the confidence that girl was taking in him. It seemed to her that all her gestures were covered with a

[

studied spontaneity, and she thought it was probably Daniel's ex.

—Ah, then I still have a chance..." Andrea smiled and pulled Daniel close to her, holding him by the waist in an overly affectionate way.

—Whenever you want, you're like a bedbug, Andrea," he rebuked her with a smile as he gently pushed her away.

—And what brings you here? —asked Andrea, with a face of resignation that would make a naughty girl who doesn't indulge her whims.

—We have come to talk to your father.

The door of the room opened at that moment, and on the threshold a distinguished man of about fifty—something years appeared.

—Was someone talking about me? —he said, smiling.

—Hugo! —exclaimed Daniel.

The man approached Daniel and gave him a warm hug. He was a big man, with greasy gray hair, bushy eyebrows shading his lively eyes, and a thick, neat moustache. He wore expensive clothes and his manners were exquisite. After greeting Daniel, he kissed Camila's hand gallantly and invited them to sit down.

—What's the pleasure in that? —he asked once they had all taken their seats.

—You see, Hugo," Daniel went straight to the point, "I wanted to talk to you about some packages I received.

Camila noticed how Hugo Areilza's populated eyebrow slightly furrowed when she heard those words. The businessman didn't say anything, but he repeatedly tweaked his moustache, and Camila had the impression that he was having trouble keeping his hands to himself.

Daniel explained in broad strokes to him and his daughter the story of the four boxes and their contents.

—Did you go to the police to report it? —asked Areilza when Daniel finished his story.

—The truth is that I preferred to investigate on my own before doing so.

—You've done very well," said Areilza thoughtfully. These things are immediately leaked to the press and it's not good for the image of the business...

—Do you think it might have something to do with the suicides that have been happening? —No. —asked Andrea with a worried look. They say that the suicides had also received some packages...

—I don't really know," Daniel replied seriously, looking at Areilza. —Actually... I was hoping that maybe you could tell me something.

—Me?" asked the surprised man.

Daniel left the leaflet he had taken from the reception desk on the table and kept silent. It had the name of a transport company printed on it with the logo of a black shark. Areilza looked at Daniel with a disconcerted expression. It seemed that he didn't know what they were talking about.

—We think it was a man from your company who sent the packages to Daniel," Camila intervened.

—Are you accusing my father of something? — asked Andrea indignantly.

—I'm simply saying that there's a guy who drives a company truck, who knocked Daniel out the other day," replied Camila with determination.

—You should find yourself some friends with a bit more class, Dani," exclaimed Andrea angrily.

—Like the one you have, perhaps? —Camila challenged her.

[

—Who do you think you are, coming here to insult us?

—Let's go, Andrea," measured Hugo Areilza, "don't make a fuss, nobody here has accused anybody of anything. —And turning to Daniel he added: "To tell you the truth, I can't give you any information about it, Daniel. I have dozens of employees all over the country... I can, however, do one thing. Give me the license plate number of the truck you're talking about and I'll find out who was driving it the day you were assaulted.

—Well, that would be helpful... —Daniel agreed.

—And you're saying you have no idea who might have taken those photos? —I don't. —It seems that it must have been someone very close...

—No..., I've been thinking about it, but I can't think who...

—It is a pity that your brother is no longer here," exclaimed the businessman suddenly, looking at Daniel. He could have helped us solve the mystery... He had a privileged head...

Daniel thought he sensed a slight twinkle in Areilza's dark eyes when he said these words. He didn't understand why he was mentioning his brother now; as far as he knew, they had never gotten along particularly well.

—You went out together, didn't you? —Camila suddenly asked Andrea.

—Didn't your boyfriend tell you? —she said in a haughty tone.

—He's not my boyfriend," repeated Camila.

—So, you don't care whether we go out or not.

—I was just saying that because a girlfriend is someone very close..., someone who has access to her boyfriend's privacy...

—What are you implying?

[

—Come on, girls, calm down," Areilza said again between the two of them. Then he looked at Daniel with a hurt expression and said, "Daniel, you are like a son to me. You must realize that it's not very appropriate for you and your friend to come and insinuate that we have something to do with sending the packages.

—It's possible," admitted Daniel. But you must realize that the circumstances point in this direction...

Areilza remained silent for a few seconds and stared at Daniel as if he were weighing the possibility of trusting him with something. Then he looked at his daughter and said:

—"I have a confession to make...

—Dad...? —exclaimed Andrea, perplexed.

The businessman looked at Daniel again, sighed resignedly, got up from his seat and went to a cupboard. He opened it with a key in his pocket and took out a medium—sized square box that Daniel recognized immediately.

—Are the boxes you received like this? —he asked.

[

CHAPTER 11

On the road again...	n	the	road	again...
Just can't wait to get on

On the road again. As the song says, it was difficult for Daniel to go long without rolling on the asphalt and any—any excuse was good enough to do so. In this case, the excuse had been a request from Camila. When she left the Bildex headquarters, she had asked her to leave the country. He only had one package left to receive and that would be the last, so if they were out, they couldn't deliver it. He was not afraid, but he was touched by the concern of his friend and thought it was a good opportunity to make another trip with her. Now they were crossing the Andes and their destination was Mendoza in the neighboring country.

The road climbed steep peaks, and as they climbed the air became colder, but it was so clean that, despite the altitude, it filled their lungs completely. Before them there was a magnificent landscape, difficult to imagine. It was as if every kilometer they advanced brought them a little closer to God. Camila was driving ahead, and Daniel could see her surrounded by snowy peaks cut out in a sky so blue it seemed unreal. The ascent required caution because the winds were strong there and could unbalance the bike, but both she and he were experienced bikers and knew how to take his pulse precisely at every stage of the journey. The biker was on the bike and on the road as if machine, rider and road were one and the same thing, a unique movement flowing harmoniously across the landscape. The white, silky clouds seemed to fray on the steep peaks, as if the

[

huge masses of eroded rock were children wanting to catch cotton candy.

Above the rhythmic sound of the engines, the echoes of the wind between the cliffs whispered ancient secrets to them as they passed.

Daniel watched Camila dodging the slopes of the road with gentle movements and getting ahead of any obstacle that the road might present, small oil stains or some hole or gravel to get around, as if she had done nothing else all her life. He liked that girl, and her biker skills only increased her charms, but there was something behind those beautiful eyes, a secret, a shadow of sadness whose origin he was unable to decipher. She knew she had feelings for him, of that there was no doubt: her concern that nothing should happen to him showed it. When, after Areilza's confession, she knew definitively that Daniel's life was in danger, she had not ceased until she had convinced him to leave the country. Hugo Areilza confessed to them that he himself had received four packages and was waiting for the fifth. The contents of the first three boxes coincided with those of Daniel's boxes; not so with the fourth. In the fourth package, Areilza didn't receive any photos, but a charred wooden figure that seemed to represent a little man with his arms down. He told them he didn't understand what those strange shipments meant, but he hadn't gone to the police because he didn't want the publicity for all that to spill over to his company. He said he preferred to handle it his own way. He also told them that the three suicides were the three partners in the conglomerate of companies that included Daniel's. This left no doubt that the sender of all the boxes was the same and that the link between the recipients was the corporation they had in common. Five partners, five boxes each. If nobody prevented things

[

from continuing to happen according to the same pattern, the next suicide would be Areilza or Daniel himself. Both Andrea and Camila had been keen to bring the matter to the attention of the police immediately, but they had refused. Areilza, for the reasons given, and Daniel, because there was something that didn't fit the story. Specifically, the photographs that had been sent to him. If all this was a conspiracy hatched years ago to sink the company, why hadn't Areilza received photographs as well?

They went on their way as fast as the traffic would allow and, after lunch in Portillo, they continued their journey to customs. On the other side of the border, the pace of the march accelerated, as the gentle slopes and wide curves allowed traffic to flow more smoothly. On the right side of the march, the Mendoza River was flowing quietly. On the left, behind the colorful crests of the massifs, the majestic southern slope of the Aconcagua, the highest mountain in the continent, could be seen on that day. Accompanied by its distant presence and the changing colors of the hills bathed by the evening light, they reached Mendoza. When they entered the city, Daniel thought that he would not mind running away from the packages and from the whole world together with Camila, each one with his motorbike, without needing anything else than new roads to be discovered and different landscapes to travel.

They looked for a small hotel in a central area and, once again, asked for separate beds. Daniel hadn't finished harassing them, but he knew how to get rid of the anger that was appearing inside him in time. After all, Camila had the right to make her own decisions. Once in the room, they decided to take a shower and then go to dinner.

[

While Camila was taking a shower, Daniel opened the box of photographs and spread them on his bedspread. Since he had shown them to Camila he had never looked at them again. For some reason, while he was with her, he preferred not to think about that, that strange piece of his past that he didn't know, that he didn't know how he fit into what he thought he had experienced so far. He did not trust Areilza. Although it was a person who had always got along quite well with him, his brother Benjamin had never really liked. Daniel had always attracted these differences not so much to personal dislike, but to opposite ways of seeing the company, since his older brother, unlike him, was involved in running the family business. But now there were several things that didn't fit. Firstly, the difference between the contents of the latest packages. Then the damn yellow truck. It couldn't be a coincidence that it belonged to Areilza's fleet. He began to think that it was very likely that Areilza himself had organized everything. It could even be that, when they met at Bildex headquarters, he had invented that he was also receiving packages to divert attention from what they were talking about there: the fact that one of his employees had attacked Daniel. He thought that maybe Areilza was looking for some way, which he could not imagine, to take control of the whole business conglomerate, eliminating the other partners. Daniel clicked his tongue and shook his head in a gesture of annoyance. If he hadn't been so oblivious to the affairs of the family business, perhaps he would have had more answers now. He looked at the pictures scattered on the bed. There was something about them that was strange to him, but he could not identify it. He sensed that he was missing something, that these photos followed a common thread that ran through them, that connected them in some way, but it did not jump out

[

at him, as if it were hidden in his images. He looked at them again, one by one, he looked at his face, at his position, at the places where they had been taken... He even tried to find the moment of the day when they were taken, either by the fact that they were taken with artificial light or with natural light, or by the presence of some clock. He decided, at last, to classify them chronologically, from the first to the last, trying to locate the approximate moment when they were taken. Truly, there was much work to be done.

—Looking at family photos?

Daniel turned and saw Camila wrapped in a towel fresh from the shower. Her hair was wet, like the day they bathed together in Lake Villarrica, and a few drops were running down the slope of her skin. She had to breathe a couple of times before she could answer.

—I'm trying to find some clue in the photos, something that might give me information about who took them," he said with a slight cough.

—I wish I could help you," she replied, standing beside him so he could look at the pictures.

Daniel's gaze slipped, like the drops, over Camila's body. His brown skin contrasted with the white of the towel and gave off a soft, pleasant smell. Then he looked at her shoulder and discovered a small tattoo that he hadn't noticed the night of Lake Villarrica, perhaps because of the lack of light or the excess of alcohol. It was a rhombus with geometrical figures inscribed inside, among which two smaller rhombuses stood out, one on each side. He reached out and touched it.

—I didn't notice your tattoo," he said. "What is it?

—It's a Mapuche symbol," she said, "representing the eyes, which are the means of seeing the soul.

[

Daniel stared at her and she thought he was looking at her as if it was the first time he had ever done so.

—Do you know that your eyes are constantly changing colors?

—he asked.

—They told me," she replied with a smile, "but I can't see it well, because they can't look at themselves.

Daniel laughed at the idea and then got a little more serious.

—If the eyes are the means to see the soul..." he said, "by looking into Camila's eyes, then I can see your soul, but what I see in it is not what you tell me...

—I have another tattoo," she replied, uncomfortable with the direction the conversation was taking, "look.

The girl showed him her calf. In it, a flock of birds was flying up to the sky. Simple, elegant silhouettes represented the birds.

—And this means something? —asked Daniel, admiring the delicate shapes that furrowed Camila's skin.

—They mean the desire for freedom...

Daniel gently caressed the birds drawn on Camila's leg, and she let herself be made. He felt the warmth of the skin and the soft touch through his fingertips and slid them slowly up his thigh. Then she gently stepped back and asked him.

—You don't have any?

Daniel smiled and took off his shirt. His naked torso was empty, and Camila looked up and down at him, looking for a sign. He was excited to see her looking down on his body and seemed to perceive desire in her eyes. He turned and left his back exposed. He felt the whole process in which they were showing each other their inscribed skins, as a kind of ritual, as an intimate

[

interchange that went beyond simple curiosity. On Daniel's right shoulder blade there was a majestic tree that beautifully curled its branches and roots. Camila placed her fingers on the tattoo, just as he had done before on hers, and began to gently trace the contours of the figure. Daniel felt a chill at the soft, silky touch of her skin.

—It's a powerful image," said Camila behind him.

Does it have any meaning?

—It's the tree of life, he said. For me it is very important, it means my earthly connection with the spiritual.

She didn't answer but continued to wander through the inky forms in silence, like a light, minimal caress that lasted for a long time. Daniel closed his eyes and let himself be carried away by that caress without saying anything, feeling the girl's breath on his back and the touch of his fingers on his skin. Two or three minutes could go by like that, until he noticed how her fingertips were separating, and it seemed to him as if a current that had been circulating between the two of them during that time suddenly broke.

—Go take a shower," proposed Camila, "and I'll have a look at the pictures too.

Daniel went into the bathroom, turned on the cold water in the shower and let the jet fall on his body. He was boiling with desire inside. Those few minutes when he hadn't even seen Camila, but had felt her just behind him, had excited him even more than when he held her in his arms at the lake. He felt his muscles contract with the contact of the cold water running through his body, and at the same time his inner fire slowly died down. He thought that when he left the bathroom he would tell Camila to leave him, that they could not be friends, but the next moment he erased that idea from his head. He didn't want to imagine a world without the changing color of those eyes. He hit the shower base in a rage. He had to find out what the hell was going on with that girl, what her pain was. Then he thought he heard something through the noise of the water jet and turned off the faucet.

—Daniel, look at this! —he heard behind the bathroom door.

He dried himself as best he could, wrapped himself in the towel as a loincloth and went quickly into the room.

—I think I've found something..." said Camila excitedly with some photos in her hand. "Look, here," she pointed to a spot on one of the photos.

—I don't understand... —he said. It's just the lighter on the table.

—And here, she pointed to another photo.

—The lighter, next to a beer bottle... You mean all the pictures show the lighter?

—I thought so at first," she replied with an excited tone in her voice, "because it was in many of the pictures.

But when I didn't see it in all of them, I looked at the other pictures for something related. Look!

It's a T—shirt...

—Yes, but look at the symbol on it.

—It's the anchored cross. Yes, I told you it was my brother's badge... It's an old shirt of his that I keep.

—In the pictures where the lighter doesn't come out, the shirt comes out.

—You mean that of the 40 or 50 photos there are, there isn't one that doesn't have one of these two things?

—Exactly! —replied Camila triumphantly.

—And what's the point of that?

[

101]

—Think," she said. The common denominator of these two objects is the anchored cross. What does that cross mean?

—No! —I don't think that's it! —exclaimed Daniel as if a light suddenly shone in his head. The common denominator is my brother! They were both his things!

—But... that makes everything even stranger... — What can that mean? What relationship can the photos have with your brother?

—Maybe someone is sending me a message...

Daniel walked thoughtfully to the window and put his arms on the sill. He looked up at the sky and thought of Benjamin. A lump in his throat formed and he felt a bitterness coming from inside mixing with an early rage. Who the hell had been playing with his brother's memory? He took a deep breath in the afternoon air from the city, trying to clarify his thoughts. He looked down at the square where children were playing ball. His gaze wandered over the trees in front, the stone fountain in the center, the grey facades due to pollution, and the vehicles parked on the sides. Suddenly he stopped at one of them and all the rage that had been concentrated in his heart was automatically directed at what he was looking at. Right in front of him, next to the children playing and the passers—by passing by, he had parked a yellow tanker.

[

CHAPTER 12

Edmundo Calleja had dined magnificently; that little restaurant near the hotel had been a real find. He was heading to his truck, satisfied, smoking a cigar and enjoying the nightly ride. He loved to start his digestion by tasting the tobacco smoke, let it stay in his mouth and lungs for a while, and then gently expel it. The night was splendid, and the stars shone in the Mendoza night sky. He opened the cabin door and took out a detective novel which he had left in the glove compartment, and before going to sleep he would read a little. With his fingernail he extracted a residue of food which had been left between his teeth and scratched his head over his black jockey, as he gazed at the yellow surface of his truck for a long time. He decided that as soon as he had time he would clean it up again. He liked to keep it spotless, it was almost an unhealthy obsession with the care of his truck. The trip from Santiago to Mendoza had covered the tank with a thin layer of dust, the fenders and the tires were somewhat muddy. But he would soon fix that. He gently stroked the tank, as if caressing a mare's belly. He would leave the vehicle sleeping there; if he hadn't been fined yet, it wasn't likely that he would be fined during the night. The next day he would move it. The important thing was not to lose sight of Daniel Balmaceda's. He closed the door of the truck well and went to his hotel, which was located about two hundred meters away. As he got into the elevator he thought about his prey. Surely he was a spoiled guy, the typical rich kid who has never lacked anything. He spat on the elevator floor in a rage. But the man didn't have bad taste, he thought: the girl who was with him was there to take his breath away. If he could just grab her... When he entered the room, he took off his shoes and sat down on the bed. He would read for a while and go to sleep soon; the next day he wanted to get up early so that the two chicks wouldn't escape.

There was a knock at the door; someone was knocking.

He hadn't asked for anything at the reception desk and those were not hours. Tomorrow he would complain to the receptionist. He got up cursing to himself and opened the door. Then it was as if the world fell in on him. Without seeing it coming, he received a blow to the face that knocked him down on the floor bleeding with a split lip. Surprised as well as hurt, he tried to see who his attacker was.

—Daniel! —He heard a woman's voice from the ground, still half stunned by the blow. Please! You told me there would be no violence!

—This son of a bitch is going to tell us what he wants from me!

Then he recognized Daniel Balmaceda's. She was standing in front of him, her face unraveled, out of her mind. Behind him was the girl, holding his arm, as if trying to restrain him. "Damn son of a bitch," he thought, as he held on to his chin that had been injured by the punch, "now you're going to find out.

—You've got the wrong man, boy," he said as he tried to get up and hit back. Suddenly he felt his forehead being held by a gun.

Balmaceda's had taken a revolver out of his jacket and was pointing it at his head at close range.

—Daniel! —Are you out of your mind? —He heard the girl scream.

Edmundo Calleja's pulse quickened and he felt a cold sweat drench his forehead. He had never had a gun to his head before.

—Listen, boy, calm down, we can talk about it," he mumbled, swallowing his saliva.

—Calm down, you bastard? —shouted Balmaceda's more and more nervously. Tell me why you sent me the packages...

Or I'll unlock the whole magazine for you!

Calleja noticed that Balmaceda's hand was shaking. She couldn't tell if it was from fear, from inexperience or from her own anger. In any case, she thought it was not good.

—Listen, I have nothing to do with this story.

—Who from? —asked Balmaceda's, pointing the gun at him.

—I can't tell you that. I'm risking my neck," he replied in a muffled voice, feeling the muzzle of the gun on his skin.

—You won't have your neck on the line if you don't sing," threatened Balmaceda's in increasing excitement.

—Do what you like," said Calleja as a pearl of sweat slipped down his temple.

—You wanted it, you bastard! —replied Balmaceda's, cocking his gun. The click that sounded when he pulled the hammer back with his thumb rumbled in Calleja's ears as if amplified, as if its sound spread throughout the room like a harbinger of death.

—I... —I can't! —pleaded Calleja, her mouth dry with anxiety.

—Please don't do this, Daniel, this isn't like you! — shouted the girl holding Balmaceda's free arm.

—You don't know what I'm like! —shouted this one more and more after the tornado, as he pushed her into the ground. He wouldn't be the first!

The girl sobbed on the hotel carpet, desperate. The pressure of the gun on Calleja's forehead was

The call of the road

becoming unbearable for him. Kneeling on the floor, his legs began to shake.

—All right... —You win! —He shouted, "I'll tell you anything you want to know!

Calleja, prostrate and defenseless in that position, admitted to Daniel that he had taken the package to the bar on the road, but assured him he knew nothing about any other package. He confessed to her that it was also him who had hit her when he realized she was following him. He explained to her that he worked at the transport company in Areilza and that from time to time he did some small jobs for his boss, outside of his duties as a truck driver. Apparently, Areilza had asked him to deliver that package to the bar and to follow Daniel's movements from a distance. To do this, she had hidden a GPS locator on Daniel's bike so that he could determine his position simply by looking at his cell phone with an application to track the location of the device. Her instructions were to track Daniel's activity, see where he was going, if he was meeting someone, etc., and provide that information to Hugo Areilza. But I had no idea what this one wanted it for.

—I swear I don't know anything else," said Calleja with a lump in her throat, because Daniel had never taken the gun barrel off his forehead.

—Are you sure you have nothing to do with the other packages?

—I don't know what other packages you're talking about, I swear. If I knew, why wouldn't I tell you if I've already admitted that I delivered a package?

Daniel looked at Calleja thoughtfully for a few seconds, then he carefully unscrewed the gun and took it off his head.

—If I find out you lied to me, I swear I'll come back and finish what I left halfway through the night," he said, turning around and leaving the room.

—I'm... I'm very sorry," excused the girl with tears in her eyes, and she left the room behind Balmaceda's, closing the door behind her.

Calleja, still on her knees, noticed her sphincters relaxing and a warm liquid ran down her thigh soaking into her pants.

CHAPTER 13

S Camila and Daniel still couldn't stop laughing, itting on one of the beds in their hotel room, and they had been doing so ever since they left Calleja's hotel.

—I can't believe it went so well," said Camila, wiping a tear from the back of her hand.

—You're an accomplished actress," congratulated Daniel, amusingly, and then, composing a horrified expression on his face, he imposed his voice to mimic Camila: "Please don't do it, Daniel, you're not like that!

She laughed out loud, took the toy gun they had bought a few hours earlier and pointed it at her friend's head, she said in the most guttural voice she could get:

—If I find out you've been lying to me, I swear I'll come back... Daniel, unable to contain his hilarity, embraced Camila laughing heartily. When they discovered the truck, they came up with the plan. They went to a toy store and bought the most realistic weapon they could find. Then they waited for the trucker to return to his truck in a place where they could see without being seen. They followed him to the hotel where he was staying, and from then on, everything rolled off. Now Daniel had Camila laughing in his arms. The tension of those days had reached its peak in Calleja's room, and now it was pouring out of their bodies in the form of uncontrollable laughter. Then Daniel and Camila realized that they were very close, face to face, looking into each other's eyes. They barely gave a couple more hiccups and the laughter stopped. They stood there panting, looking at each other without turning away from each other. Daniel felt Camila's fresh breath so close that he could smell its

[

sweet aroma and wanted to taste the mouth that was exhaling it. For a few seconds they stood like this, very close, looking at each other, still, as if the world had stopped around them. Then Camila moved aside, got up from her bed, and stretched out a little as if to loosen her muscles. Daniel felt as if a magical moment had broken abruptly.

—It was... it was really exciting," he said. her.

—Yes, he agreed. —I've never done anything like that before.

—Don't you think you've gone a little overboard with the punching?

—Camila scolded him with a smile.

—We had to make it true so that she would believe it.

—he excused himself. Besides, I owed him for the blow he gave me.

—Maybe you're right," she admitted, "it was a very good idea that I tried to stop you.

—Yeah, you did great," Rio Daniel. He was a bit like the bad cop and the good cop... I think that's what made the whole thing so credible...

—Yes," agreed Camila. Now we have to draw the conclusions from all this," she added a little more seriously as she sat on the bed next to her.

—The truth is that, if we think about it, this may have become more complicated than it has been made clear," said Daniel reflecting, caressing the surface of the wound on his left hand, which seemed to be starting to heal. If this guy has told us the truth, it turns out that the packages weren't sent by the same people. —He scratched his head in confusion. That's partly the same as Areilza's version. And it would force us to look for two reasons: one for the strange packages and another for the package in the photos...

[

—Already..." admitted Camila thoughtfully. But there is also the possibility that the bastard Areilza has lied to us...

—I don't think so," he denied, "I was really scared.

—Yes, that's true," smiled Camila, remembering the look of fear on Calleja's face when Daniel had put the gun to her forehead. But it's also possible that he didn't know anything

—You mean Areilza's the one who organized the packages, but the guy in the truck was only asked to deliver one?

—It's a hypothesis, —she proposed.

—It's possible," conceded Daniel, "and that would be much better for us, because then we could clear up everything by directing our shot at one bird.

—What's the next move then? —asked Camila.

—Tomorrow we'll go back to Chile and pay Hugo a visit. It's hard to believe how that bastards had me fooled all these years!

Then Daniel realized that something wasn't right. In Camila's eyes, the gleam of laughter from just a few moments ago had suddenly been clouded by a veil of sadness.

—Is something wrong? —she asked.

—No, nothing...

—Are you still afraid for me? —I am. —said Daniel.

—Yes...

—But now we are closer to the truth,' he said, approaching her and taking her gently by the shoulders. If we can find out whose fault this is, and for the moment the circumstances point to Areilza, we can expose him and go to the police.

—Yes, I know," she said unconvincingly. But I don't know, I'm not sure... Maybe... Why don't... why don't we

[

go away from here, far, far away... to Europe? — Immediately after saying those words she seemed to repent and looked away from Daniel's eyes.

—Do you really want to go with me to Europe? —he asked, caressing her cheek.

—I don't... I don't know... It was silly..." she said in astonishment.

—Listen," he reassured her, "nothing has to happen. I know we left Chile because you thought it would be safer outside the country. But you have seen that we have been followed up to here... We have to go back to Santiago and make a second visit to the Titanium Tower. It's the only way we can get to the bottom of this once and for all.

—I know..." she admitted in a whisper. But it just seems to me that every day that passes comes closer to be the last...

Daniel smiled softly at him. He pulled back a hair from her forehead and decided to come clean with her.

—Camila, I... —I don't know what's happened these days. I had sworn not to hit on any woman, at least not for a while...

—Daniel..." she began to say, but he shut his mouth by gently placing a finger over his lips.

—Let me talk, please," she said. This is costing me..." Camila nodded.

—After I broke up with Andrea," he continued, "I haven't had any other serious relationships, and I had promised myself it would take a while to get back together. I wanted to be free, to roam alone, when I wanted and how I wanted, without having to give accounts to anyone. —He stopped for a moment and looked at her, as if trying to choose carefully the words he was going to say, and took a breath before continuing. But since I have known you, something has been stirring inside me. I have felt a lot of confused emotions. I don't know if it's because of the pictures, or the packages, or why, but there you are always. You on your bike. Riding the roads. In front of me... and... and... it's been a long time since I felt as happy as I did when we rode together... you and me, on the asphalt...

—Daniel..." she repeated barely in a whisper.

—Listen," he interrupted. You said it yourself. We have a song together, remember? When the road turns, I get carried away... Well, I get carried away by you, I get carried away by that song, by the music of the road we sang together. You and I...

—Yes," she said sadly, "you and I sang a song. But you're singing a song you don't know the name of...

—What do you mean? —he asked.

She was silent as she looked out of the window, from which you could see the waning moon in the night sky.

—I only know one thing, Camila," he said, "and that's that I can't go on like this. I'm asking you to hold on to me, to squeeze me with all your strength and not let me escape... Or, if you can't do it, to let me go, to set me free... to let me go...

Camila looked at Daniel in shock and when she felt the tears well up in her eyes, she lowered her head and remained silent.

He, repeating the intimate and tender gesture with which he had taken her chin the day before, held her gently again and raised her face to look into her eyes. Moistened by the tears, they were even more beautiful, and Daniel felt a sharp pain in his chest as he looked at them. She didn't look away, she stood still, helpless, like a little hare caught in a trap, unable to move. He had her there, just a few inches away from him, and he thought they were too close to stay like that, at that minimum distance, for a long time. That this proximity could only be resolved in two ways: either by removing his hand from his face and moving away from it or by moving closer. He chose the latter and began to bring his lips closer to Camila's. Camila remained still, as if she could do nothing to avoid receiving that kiss, as if, despite her desire to prevent it, something in that situation, in the room, in her own destiny, prevented her from moving away.

Suddenly there was a knock at the door. For the second time in a short time Daniel felt the magic breaking down and looked angrily at the place where the interruption was coming from. It was a bit far— fetched, as if some evil little genie was playing a trick on him, allowing him to get close to the desired fruit that would satisfy his hunger, allowing him to reach out to the tree from which it hung and brush it with his fingers, to knock it away without warning. He almost seemed to hear the laughter of that evil spirit.

—I hope it's something important," he grunted, heading for the door.

—Wait! —she stopped him with her hand, "We don't know who he is.

Camila approached the bed and handed Daniel the toy gun. He noticed the fear in her eyes, took the gun and approached the door cautiously. Once there he asked:

—Who is it?

—Reception service, sir," said a voice behind the door, in which they immediately recognized the bellman who had shown them his room. There is mail for you.

Daniel exchanged a strange look with Camila, hid the revolver in his back trouser pocket and opened the door.

[

—This has arrived for you, sir," said the bellboy with a friendly smile, as he handed her a package wrapped in brown paper. It wasn't the first time that Daniel had seen a package exactly like that, and as he took the small box in his hands, he thought perhaps it was true what folk wisdom said: No matter how hard one tries, no one can escape their fate.

CHAPTER 14

A charred doll with its arms down, just as Areilza had told us," said Daniel, contemplating the enigmatic figure he was holding with some apprehension between his fingers. But in his case it came in package number four and in mine it's already the fifth package...

—Maybe he wasn't lying... —Planned Camila thoughtfully.

—Or maybe she was," Daniel said. If he was going to send me this package, he knew its contents beforehand. He simply had to tell me that he had received a package with similar contents to the one he was going to send me.

—But what was the point of that? If in the end it's your death he's after, then why all these packages?

—That's what we have to find out," said Daniel, placing the doll on the table in the room and wiping off the bits of soot he had left on his fingers.

Then, after thinking about his words for a moment, he added: "And we should do it soon, because this is my last package.

—You must... you must go," said Camila. "Go away... to Europe... to Canada.

—Go? —asked Daniel. "Is it not "go" anymore?

—No," she answered, going to the window and letting the night air caress her face. Go by yourself and don't tell me where you're going.

—Listen," said Daniel, approaching her and taking her by the waist, "before, just when there was a knock at the door, it seemed to me

—Please, Daniel," she interrupted him without turning around.

I can't... you don't understand...

[

—Well, explain it to me," he said tenderly.

—I can't," she replied, gazing at the waning moon, which at the time was hiding part of her visible face behind a building. You told me before to take you or let you go. —She turned to him and looked him sadly in the eyes. Okay, I'll let you go.

—This doesn't have to be," he protested. But his protest came without force, with a hint of exhaustion in his voice that he did not expect her to change her mind.

—I have been very selfish in giving you hope," she said, breaking away from him and going to the bed where the pictures were still spread out. He took one of them and stood there looking at it in silence.

—Is there anyone else? —he asked, leaning on the window sill and looking out as if he didn't want to see her, as if looking at that woman who he knew would not be his would hurt him.

—It's not that," she replied. It's not that," she replied.

—It doesn't matter," he said. "We're old enough to know what we want. You on your side and I on mine.

—Please leave Chile," she insisted.

—Don't start," he grumbled. If you don't want to have anything to do with my life, let me make my own decisions.

Camila preferred to keep quiet. She stared silently at the photos above the bed. There was nothing she could say to Daniel to ease his pain, so she preferred to try to trick his own pain by diverting his mind to something else. He put it in the pictures in front of him. What could they mean? What relationship could they have with Daniel's brother if, as he said, that was the connection between them? For his part, Daniel could think of nothing. Anger ran through his body. He wanted to get

[

out of there immediately and never see Camila again, to go downstairs, pay for the hotel and go back to Santiago on his motorbike that night. He even had the idea of going to Hugo Areilza's house, getting him out of bed and beating him up until he confessed everything. Then he realized that he was delirious. He wasn't like that. He wasn't a bully. He needed to calm down. He took a cigarette out of his packet and put it in his mouth. He stroked his fingertip over the initials and the cross inscribed on the Zippo and felt the pain knot in his throat. He lit the cigarette and inhaled the smoke deeply, held it in his lungs for a moment and then exhaled it into Mendoza's night, as if he wanted to expel with it all the weight accumulated in his heart. The smoke came between her eyes and the moon, which was barely visible behind the façade of the building which hid her. After a few moments, the smallest section of the white disc was completely hidden, leaving a shining blue halo as the only testimony of its presence. The square, which had been lit up until now, was tinged with a dimmer, yellowish light from the street lights that surrounded it. Daniel looked at the empty square. There were no more people, no more noises, no more children playing around. Even the jet from the fountain had stopped flowing. It seemed to him to be a metaphor for what was happening inside. The rage he felt at not being able to know, not understanding what the pain of that girl was, what the reason was for her refusal to obey her heart, had given way to unbearable pain and despondency. He felt her behind him, on the bed, but he did not want to look at her. She was like the moon, hidden from his eyes, no longer offering him her light. He thought it would be unbearable to look at her again. But he could not stay all his life looking at that silent and empty square. He took another puff and dropped the ashes into the void. Then he looked up at the glowing embers of his cigarette and released the smoke on it, causing a few tiny luminous sparks to break out and be lost in the air. Again, he let his tired gaze fall upon the lonely square, and then his eyes opened with surprise.

—She has disappeared! —she exclaimed.

Camila ran to the window and saw for herself. The tanker was gone.

—Why has it gone? —She asked, "Are you going to travel all night to Santiago?

—I don't know, maybe the guy's still here in Mendoza, but he's gone somewhere else so we can't reach him.

—Do you think he's the one who brought the box?

—It's possible... although... he stopped, as if he had suddenly realized something and exclaimed, "We look like idiots!

He went to the door and opened it.

—I'll be right back," he said.

—I'm coming with you, —replied Camila as she left the room with him.

—As you wish," Daniel reluctantly accepted. Anyway, we're not going very far.

They went down in the lift to the ground floor without looking at each other or talking. Once there, Camila followed Daniel to the reception, where the receptionist gave them a broad smile under his minimal, preening moustache.

—Good evening," said Daniel. We're in the room.

204. About ten or fifteen minutes ago we got a package delivered. Could you talk to the bellman who uploaded it?

The receptionist raised his eyebrows with a surprised expression.

—He didn't do anything wrong...

[

121]

—No, no," Daniel hurried to reassure him. I just wanted to ask him a few questions about the person who brought the package.

—I'm sorry," he replied, putting the kind smile back on his face. You've just left, your shift is over.

—Shit," Daniel muttered in frustration.

—You were here when they brought him in? — Camila intervened.

The receptionist looked at her as if she knew she was there and answered without undoing her smile.

—That's right, Miss.

—Great," exclaimed Daniel, "could you describe it to me, please?

The receptionist loosened the tension in his smile a little, as if he didn't dare erase it completely, but he raised his chin a little, as if to be able to look at his interlocutors from a certain moral distance. With his eyes he wanted to show them that he did not find this questioning relevant, but with his mouth he said:

—Of course, sir.

Then he narrowed his eyes slightly and looked at an undefined point above the customers, as if trying to remember. Daniel and Camila patiently listened to the answer, which seemed to take longer than necessary.

—I was a gentleman," he said at last.

—Couldn't you be a little more explicit? —asked Daniel, who was beginning to get impatient.

—He must have been about thirty—eight or forty years old, short dark hair, normal build," described the receptionist, trying to give the impression with every word that what they were asking him was completely out of order.

—Is there anything that characterized him, anything that could give me information about this person?

The receptionist looked at his interlocutor as if he were pushing the boundaries of reason.

—You will understand that this request is absolutely unusual,' he cleared slightly as he stroked his meagre moustache with his finger. Besides, I don't know to what extent I'm authorized to provide this kind of information...

—I know it may seem strange," Daniel rushed to improvise, "but I think this shipment was a mistake, and we would need to know the sender to return it. You'd be doing us a huge favor if you could help us.

—I'm sorry, sir, I can't think of anything else to say.

—Was he wearing a uniform? —Was he wearing a dog tag?

—No, sir. He was wearing civilian clothes.

—Let's go, Camila," snorted Daniel irritably, giving up, "we're not going to get anything out of it here.

—It's a pity," said the woman, reaching into her trouser pocket and taking out a note she had deposited on the counter, "because that information could have been very useful... for everyone. —He said this, put his hand on the ticket, and looked meaningfully at the receptionist.

Daniel looked at her in surprise and admired the cheekiness with which she had formulated those words. He couldn't help smiling, and that smile seemed to wash away all the bitterness that had settled in him a few minutes before. He thought sadly that this girl had something that could heal his wounds in a matter of seconds. It was a pity that it was also she who inflicted them.

The receptionist's eyes glowed at the sight of the ticket.

—Now that I remember," he said, spreading a bright hyena smile on his face again, "I do remember one characteristic of the man who brought the package.

—What is it? —asked Camila without raising her hand from the money.

The receptionist looked greedily at the bill and answered:

—He was a Mapuche Indian.

Daniel looked at Camila perplexed. She looked at the receptionist and gave him the same fake smile as he did, as he took the ticket from the counter and put it back in his pocket.

—He said, 'You have been a great help to us. Good night," he said.

—Good evening,' said the receptionist, trying to hide behind his faded smile the anger and bewilderment he felt at the time.

Once in the room, Daniel and Camila were talking about the peculiarity of the messenger: a Mapuche Indian. This people spread across large areas in Southern Chile and also, though to a lesser extent, in Argentina, which made it possible to suppose that the Indian who brought the package might be Argentinian. Anyway, that was unlikely; most likely it was a simple messenger of whoever was making the shipments, so maybe it was a Chilean Indian who had gone there with the only mission of making the delivery. But how did he know he was there? Had he followed them as well as Callejas did? It was getting more and more confusing, but in any case, they had one more piece of information: Callejas had not been the one who had made the delivery.

Daniel felt comforted. Not because of the new information they had obtained, which had not really advanced their investigation, but because they had talked to Camila again as if nothing had happened. That had happened more than once between them. In spite of being angry, any small event, however small, made them immediately forget their anger, and they shared the same complicity and good humor as always. They were a good team, Daniel thought what one could not do, the other did, and when one did not know how to move forward, the other came up with a way out. They complemented each other perfectly, not only because of their love of the road, but, in general, because of their way of seeing life and facing it. That's why it was even more painful to lose her. In any case, he decided not to mention that night's dispute again. He didn't want to let her out of his sight. At least not yet. He still had some hope that she would change her mind, or at least give him a reason why she could not be with him. He decided to stay by her side at least until the mystery of the boxes was solved. Or until that mystery killed him...

—But if the guy in the truck didn't do it, then maybe Areilza told us the truth," Camila said.

—I don't think so," Daniel objected, "he could have sent his henchman to watch us and the other guy to make the delivery. That explains it," he said, "it would be better if they knew we were here. I find it hard to believe that there are so many people following us. They would have had to put another GPS on the bike to detect our movements or have followed us closely from Santiago...

—Yes, you're right," admitted Camila, "it seems an absurd idea. Besides, we know Areilza lied to us, since he was the one who sent the fourth package. If he lied to us about one thing, he could have lied about everything.

At that moment Daniel's cell phone rang.

[

—I think we're going to find out soon," he said, looking at the screen where the call came from. It's Andrea.

Daniel answered, and from the way his expression changed, Camila knew something wasn't right.

—I'm really sorry, Andrea," said Daniel at last. I'm in Argentina now, but as soon as I can I'll go there... Yes, of course... And anything else you need, you know... A big kiss.

When Daniel hung up, Camila didn't need to ask what had happened. Yet she looked at him without saying anything, hoping that he would confirm her fears.

—Areilza has committed suicide, said Daniel. He was wearing a bird mask.

CHAPTER 15

O bikers. The one who seemed to have the n the way back to Chile they found a group of leading voice, Manuel, a guy in his early fifties, with long prophet's beards, a golden earring and a magnificent custom—made Kawasaki in bright colors, invited them to share the road. "Like brothers of the road," he said with a nice laugh. Although Daniel had always been a free rider, a steppe wolf who liked to wander around and just follow his own instincts, he also enjoyed the gregariousness of the biker's inclination, the feeling of being surrounded by the warmth of the pack. One of the first things he learned when he started riding his bike was something taught to him by an experienced old biker whom he met in a roadhouse and who reminded him a little of the eccentric Manuel: there was an important difference between a biker and a motorcyclist. The former is someone who rides a motorcycle, and there everyone who drives a car stays, who can more or less enjoy the ride, but roughly speaking all he does is use a means of transport to get from one place to another. The second, the motorcyclist, is someone who merges with the bike, who in a way has made his life that riding the road, to the point that he no longer conceives of one thing without the other. He is the one who is more comfortable on a motorcycle than anywhere else, and who, from the first day he rides it, just as it happened to him, tastes the sound of freedom, which is the sound of the engine. The biker feels bewitched, overcome by the smell of petrol and asphalt as much as by the breath of a woman, and, however independent he may be, he is always ready to share that

[

habitat in which a chosen few participate, that common world that is the road, with those who know their peers.

That day, the road was clear, and they could roll in rhythm. The ascent to the Chilean border was smooth and full of nuances and colors. The summits surrounded them as they passed and seemed to greet the passing of the asphalt riders with their geological fronts. Suddenly, Manuel, who was at the head of the convoy, pointed out to them with his hand upwards, and they could see a beautiful sparrow hawk majestically furrowing the skies. It was things like that that made Daniel love life on the asphalt, opening his existence to all possibilities, never knowing what one might find. He was overcome by a solemn, almost rebellious feeling, as he watched the flight of the bird evolving on the ancient rock cut out against the sky. He felt somehow a part of it all, as if the road, his Midnight, and Nature transcended his own life and gave it a new, richer, more powerful meaning which linked him to something far greater than himself. They continued with the group until they passed the border with Chile, but, although Daniel felt the current of brotherhood that ran through the row of motorcycles, in reality he was always alone when he rode his bike. It was like in those space movies where a ship goes deep into the cosmos at ultrasonic speeds. Everything around it seems to disappear and it goes through a multi—dimensional barrier wrapped in a lot of colorful flashes. He, with his motorbike, would go into the mass of air ahead of him and sometimes, when he was riding at high speed, it was as if everything disappeared, the wheels, the road, the motorbike itself, to leave him alone with the wind, floating like that sparrow hawk you had just seen. But even when the speed was slower, riding his bike meant that Daniel was in a way moving away from the world, forcing the wind to push him, attracting the air and, as in the films of space, entering another dimension. And in that dimension, his mind seemed to move more freely, more smoothly. Thoughts, problems, worries, which normally clung to your brain like little insects, seemed to fall away, to circulate meekly in your head without landing anywhere. That journey was largely cathartic for him and allowed him, if not to forget, to suspend the threat of death hanging over his head, and to cushion a weight that gravitated over him with even more force than the fear of what might happen to him: the fear of losing Camila.

They continued on their way alone to Santiago and stopped for lunch at the way. They were impregnated with the smells of the journey, of the mountains, of oxygen, of sap, of benzine. Each little fragrance that the air brought was adhering to their memory and always, after a long journey, they retained for a long time inside all those sensations that had been impregnated by the road. Neither she nor he mentioned at any time the discussion of the previous day, as if it had never taken place. Daniel was grateful for this silence; he didn't want to direct his energies to something that seemed to have no solution and that only made him sad and depressed, which wasn't the best way to find out who had sent the packages. Time was running out; the fifth package had already been sent to him and he was the only one of the five corporate partners still alive. The conversation during the meal focused on the possible movements to be made from then on. Camila told him that he should go to the police, that there was no point in playing the hero, and that there seemed to be nowhere to hide from that terrible threat. He promised to look into it, but first

[

he wanted to investigate all the possibilities. The fact that the messenger who carried the package was of Mapuche race opened up another line of investigation, which, though weak, could shed light on the mystery. Otherwise, the meal was relaxed, and they joked and provoked each other again, as if both were trying to fight with jokes and good humor that nightmare to which destiny had dragged them.

When they arrived in the capital they went to the department of Daniel in Providencia, northwest of Santiago. They had met there with Mapuca, the woman who had been Daniel's governess as a child and who was now in charge of cleaning his house, ironing and other domestic chores.

The reason they had met her was not minor, considering the new circumstances that had appeared on the scene: she was of Mapuche descent.

—It's a great neighborhood you live in," exclaimed Camila when they parked their motorbikes. It's quite a luxury!

—Well, it's not the most elitist in Santiago," Daniel tried to play down, "although it's nice and cozy.

—Sometimes I come with friends to a local place," she said, "there are some very cool places... Maybe we've met in some dive.

—I doubt it. I wouldn't have forgotten...

Daniel regretted it right away when he said that. Things were flowing between them now, and he preferred to keep it that way. Every time mention was made of something that had to do with his feelings for her, or hers for him, a shadow seemed to rise between the two of them, which made it all seem so strange. In order not to let that shadow appear, Daniel diverted his attention from his words to another place:

[

—Look, there's my apartment," he said, pointing to a building with an entrance bordered by a perfectly cut cypress hedge with flower beds at its base.

—Wow," exclaimed Camila, "what a beautiful building!

—It's not that bad," laughed Daniel, "you'll see that inside it's not very big.

—You're going to think I'm a village girl," said Camila suddenly, a little embarrassed.

—Why would I think that?

—I don't know... —I've been to places like this before, don't you think? You're not the first rich friend I've had...

—I don't believe anything," he said, somewhat annoyed. He felt a pinch of jealousy as he thought of the meaning she would give to the word 'friend'.

—Don't listen to me," she said, blushing and looking down. Maybe I'm saying something silly... I'm tired from the trip.

Daniel thought that blush suited him very well and pulled his hair out of his face, he said:

—I like your nonsense.

They came in and greeted the doorman. The elevator was accessed with a small key that each owner had. Once inside, the key was also needed to move to the different floors. On the tenth floor, the elevator doors opened, leading directly to a small lobby in the apartment itself, which in turn gave access to a large living room. Camila recognized her immediately from the photos.

—Does one enter directly from the elevator into your apartment? —she asked, surprised.

—Yes," said Daniel. But you can also get in through a back door.

[

—And does anyone in the building have access to the elevator key? I can tell from the photos...

Daniel couldn't answer because someone suddenly emerged from a hallway. It was Mapuca, who came to him with open arms.

—How's my boy? —he said, hugging him and filling him with kisses.

—Not so young anymore, Mapuca," he replied a bit ashamed, kissing his old nanny as well.

—For me, you will always be," she said with a big smile. Then he looked at Camila without stopping smiling and asked:

And who is this beautiful girl?

Daniel made the introductions and Mapuca hugged and kissed Camila as if he had known her for years. She was a dark woman, probably In her mid—fifties, although her face was worn out and she looked more like it. Maybe life had not treated her well, Camila thought. She was a bit chubby and short, but looked like she was overflowing with energy. She wore a thick bow on the back of her neck, which gave her an elegant look, although at the time she was wearing a white apron. Her face showed her Mapuche ancestry immediately.

—Now you tell me that mysterious thing you want to tell me," said the woman, disappearing down a corridor, "but first I am going to make you some good coffee.

Daniel took the opportunity to show Camila the apartment. It was a cozy place, with designer furniture and decorated in a modern but casual way, without superfluous luxuries. The view from its windows showed a beautiful panorama of the city. Both of them took off their jackets and Camila, who was wearing a tank top, left her beautiful shoulders visible. After a while, Mapuca

[

appeared with a tray containing freshly brewed coffee, milk and an assortment of tea cookies.

It's finger—licking good, you'll see! —he said as he poured the coffee and milk into the cups.

Daniel explained the story to her without leaving out any details, but very carefully so as not to scare her as much as possible, although he knew it was inevitable that he would be affected by knowing those facts, since he loved him very much and his life was in danger. She listened attentively without interrupting at any moment, although the expression on her face changed as the story progressed and during the whole time it lasted, she was repeatedly sanctified.

—By Ngenechen! —he exclaimed when Daniel finished. And why haven't you gone to the police, my boy?

—I wanted to find out for myself what had happened

—But I don't know what they'll do either. Will they put an agent on me, guarding me around the clock? Bear in mind that there really has been no murder. All four deaths were suicides...

—I don't know, Daniel, I think you should still go to the police, —she insisted. Then, addressing Camila, he added in a pitiful tone: "Don't you think so, girl?

Camila took pity on the woman. Thousands of past bitter nesses were reflected on her face, a whole story locked in those wrinkles that seemed to be readable just by looking at her. She didn't know what she had been through in her life, since she didn't know her, but it distressed her to have to add one more pain to the pile of suffering she guessed on that face. Gently taking his remaining hand, he replied:

[

—"I've told you a thousand times, but you don't listen to me.

—If he doesn't listen to you, he'll do less to me," said Mapuca, trying to hold back a tear that was struggling to come out.

—We wanted to ask you something, Mapu," said Daniel. But first, I would like you to tell me if you can think of who has been able to take the photos during these years... You know everyone well...

Mapuca got up and went to a piece of furniture in the room, from which he extracted a bottle of liquor.

—I don't want to give your girlfriend a bad impression," he said, "but I think I need a drink now. Would you like some?

Daniel cursed to himself. Why was everyone so keen to attribute a relationship with Camila to him? They both refused the offer and Mapuca, taking a glass from a shelf in the same cabinet, poured the coppery liquid into it and took a drink. Then he went back to the table. Camila thought her face had been transfigured, as if she were someone else. The woman who watched them from that chair seemed now to be boiling with the millennial Amerindian blood coursing through her veins.

—Forget about the pictures, boy," he said in a tone of voice that could not be replied to. That's not important now. From what you've told me, they were sent by Andrei's father and he's one of the dead. You'll have time to find out who took them and why. The important thing now is that you turn your attention to the other four packages.

Camila was amazed by the lucidity and certainty with which that woman suddenly spoke. A few moments ago, she had seen her dejected and defeated, and now her face radiated strength and determination.

[

—I don't know if I'll have time to find out anything," said Daniel thoughtfully. I've already received five packages. The extra time I'm supposed to be alive is a gift...

—Don't say that," protested Camila.

—Think, boy! —I slapped the Mapuca on the table. You still haven't received the fifth package. The package with the photos doesn't count. —He took another short drink from his glass and added, "Give me one of those cigars of yours.

—If it's like you say, we still have some time," said Daniel, offering Mapuca tobacco. After giving him a light, he lit a cigarette too and left the lighter on the table. Mapuca picked it up and looked at the initials engraved on it as he expelled the tobacco smoke.

—You miss him, don't you?

—Always," answered Daniel sadly.

Mapuca looked at Daniel and finally let out that tear he had been holding back. He immediately wiped it away with the back of his hand, as if to make it clear that there was no room for such things at that time.

—What did you want to ask me? —he said.

—You know that the person who brought the fifth package... well, the fourth, if we don't count the one in the photos, was a Mapuche Indian...

—Yes.

—We wanted to know if you find any relation between the content of the packages and the Mapuche culture...

—Why do you think there might be a connection, kid? —I don't know.

—he asked with a certain irritation in his voice. It always seems that the Mapuches are to blame for something...

—It's not that, Mapuca," said Daniel, "it's that it's the only thing we have to hold on to.

—Let me think," said Mapuca, taking a puff on his cigarette and expelling from his mouth a few wisps of smoke that frayed as they ascended in the air. A spider, a chicken with its throat cut, a lot of insects and a figure of scorched wood, right?

—That's right.

The woman looked down, as if lost in thought, and stayed that way for a minute or two. Her fingers drew shapes absently with a little sugar that had been spread on the table. Finally, she looked up and said:

—I think I can make some connection between the contents of the packages and some Mapuche traditions I once heard from my grandfather. It's just supposition, of course, because I hardly remember the details, but maybe they'll help.

—Thank you, Mapuca, tell us," said Daniel with a glint of hope in his eyes.

—I'd like to ask you something first, my boy," said Mapuca, hurrying up his cigar.

—Go ahead," agreed Daniel.

—Why did you come to ask me about the Mapuches, when you have one by your side?

Daniel looked at Camila with bewilderment. Camila's beautiful eyes shone in the afternoon light that flooded the apartment with soft amber tones.

CHAPTER 16

Is that true? —Daniel asked

Camila, baffled.
Are you a Mapuche?
—No..." she answered hesitantly. Well... my grandmother belonged to the Mapuche people, but that doesn't make me one of them...
—Are you ashamed to be? —Mapuca asked with a haughty expression on his worn face.
—No, no... not at all... I just don't like to define myself... I don't think people can be put into closed categories... Camila took the cigarette from Daniel's fingers, put it in her mouth and nervously inhaled the smoke. When she released it, she added: "I am a free person and the only thing that defines me is my own actions, not a birth certificate.
—I like your philosophy," said Mapuca, relaxing a little the seriousness of his countenance.
—But... how did you know... ——asked Camila.
—The years take away the sight of the eye, but they sharpen the experience

—replied Mapuca, savoring the drink from his glass. There are small features on your face that, to an expert eye like mine, give away that blood of our people runs through your veins.

—Only because of that did you know? —Daniel asked in astonishment.

I didn't even notice!

—Well, that and a couple of other details," recognized Mapuca with a mischievous smile. The Mapuche flag sewn on the back of his jacket and the Mapuche symbol tattooed on his shoulder have helped a little...

—

You're a hell of a detective! —Daniel recognized with astonishment. We should have come to see you earlier.

—In any case," added Mapuca, casting a look of irony at Camila, "so as not to consider you a Mapuche, you seem to like the symbolism of my people very much.

The girl did not answer. She felt uncomfortable with the direction the conversation was taking. Instead of returning Daniel's cigarette after the puff, she inhaled the tobacco smoke again.

—But... —Why didn't you say anything? —he asked, taking another cigarette from the box.

—Why did I have to tell you? —I didn't. —Camila replied in a defensive tone. Did you tell me where your grandparents were from?

—Don't be angry," said Daniel holding her hand. I don't know... if we came to ask Mapuca about the Mapuches, it's only natural that you would have told me something about... about you...

—I told you I don't consider myself a Mapuche, — she said coldly as she let go of her hand. —It seems as if I've done something wrong...

—No, not at all," Daniel said quickly. It's just that...

—It's okay," she cut him off. —Can we start with the Mapuca story?

—Perfect for me," she replied, squeezing the liquor from her glass in one gulp. But listen to me carefully, young man," he said.

—Of course," agreed Daniel. We're all ears.

—My grandparents told me many stories as a child

—He began his Mapuche story, rolling his eyes as if he were going back to the very moment of his youth

[

when he heard those stories. I don't know how much truth there is in them and how much invention, because they also told me traditional tales of the Mapuche lands, and it is possible that, with time, my head has mixed some things with others, so it is not very easy for me to distinguish between them. There is, however, a tradition that I think fits in with this business of packages. —He gazed for a moment at the empty bottom of the glass in which a little drop of liquor was still glistening, as if pondering the possibility of pouring a little more alcohol. He looked for a moment at the empty bottom of the glass in which there was still a little drop of liquor glistening, and then, as if he had decided to ignore this unwelcome impulse, he continued, 'Each of the packages may symbolize a sin. The poison of the spider, the blood of the chicken, the creatures that crawl... All these things would be, according to this interpretation, expressions of evil..., something that the recipients of the packages carry in their consciousness for some reason...

—But I... —What could I have done wrong? —Daniel asked, bewildered. I've never had anything to do with the Mapuches...
—I can't tell you that," replied Mapuca, "only you can know that... Although it's also possible that it has nothing to do with you.
—What do you mean? —he asked, intrigued.
—The common thread that links the packages are the partners of the conglomerate of companies to which yours belongs," explained Mapuca thoughtfully. It is very possible that the sin has to be looked for in some act of the company more than in a specific individual?
—But I don't know anything about my company... —I've never been in the business...

[

141]

—

—Maybe the person who sent the packages doesn't know," replied a thoughtful Mapuca. Or maybe, in their eyes, that doesn't absolve you of responsibility.

You don't look like a simple cleaner," said Camila suddenly, amazed at how the Mapuche was shattering her explanations. Then, as if realizing that her eating could be interpreted as a sign of discourtesy, she added, "I don't mean that it's dishonorable to clean, or anything like that... It's just that... your way of talking... thinking... doesn't seem like that of a..." Camila took a deep breath, as if trying to find the right words. She felt like she was screwing up more and more. At the expectant gaze of Mapuca, who was waiting for her to finish her sentence, she tried to clear her thoughts before she had finished entering a dead end. Finally, he said: "Forgive me. What I really mean is that if someone told me you were a lawyer; I wouldn't be the least bit surprised.

—I thank you for the comment," said Mapuca with a smile not without a certain pride, "but many people like me have not been able to study and have had to make do with other things

—I didn't know you aspired to anything else," said a shocked Daniel, holding his old governess's hand. I thought... I thought you were happy like that...

—And I am, my boy," smiled Mapuca, placing his hand tenderly on hers. Don't get me wrong, I'm not complaining. I owe a great deal to your family and I have been very happy in their service. —He looked at Daniel with a strange look that mixed love and sadness. I'm just saying that if the circumstances had been different, maybe...

[

—But it's not too late. There's always time to do something," Daniel interrupted her. Just tell me what you need, and I'll...

—I haven't finished the story yet," she cut him, taking her hands off his and getting up again. She took the empty glass from the table and, as if she had changed her mind, went to the cabinet to refuel. And I've asked for your attention," she added as she poured out a little more liquor.

—Of course, Mapu, I'm sorry," excused Daniel, a little confused by the somewhat abrupt attitude of his old nanny.

—This is important, my boy," he said when he sat down at the table again. You're playing with it a lot...

—Life," he replied taciturnly.

—Life..." repeated Mapuca, staring at the liquld in his glass, as if he could read something in it. After a short drink he continued: "It is possible that, just as the contents of the first packages represent the sin, the contents of the last package represent the punishment.

—But what is the content of the last one? I thought that was the figure I received, but you say no, that was the fourth?

—Maybe the contents of the last package are the mask

—You told me that everyone who committed suicide died with a bird mask on, didn't you?

—Yes.

—Do you know what the bird was?

—No, we haven't seen the mask. —Why do you ask?

—If that bird represented an owl, I would be almost certain that my hypothesis is correct, —the Mapuche woman said firmly. There is a tradition that speaks of a sorcerer who takes the shape of that bird to do harm at

[

143]

—

night. And in Mapuche folklore, the bird—man carries messages from one place to another. The mask could represent a somber message... a sentence...

—We must then find out if the mask was the content of the last package and what it looked like...

—concluded Daniel.

Exactly," confirmed Mapuca. But remember that all this is just a theory...

—But that's all we have," said Daniel gloomily.

—There's something else," the Mapuche suddenly said. Do you have the last package you received here?

—Yes, downstairs on the motorbike.

—I think it's possible that if I see the figure I can confirm my suspicions.

—I'll go downstairs and get it," said Daniel, standing up from the table.

When the two women were left alone, the older one turned tenderly to the younger one.

—I'm sure I won't find anything out by telling you this, but you're very pretty.

—Thank you very much," smiled Camila, grateful for the compliment.

—You shouldn't be ashamed of your roots, my child," Mapuca continued, "he won't reject you for that... I have known him since he was no bigger than a grain of rice. —The Mapuche laughed at her own quip.

—I am not ashamed," insisted the girl. Besides, Daniel and I are just friends, we have no interest in each other... Mapuca laughed again as if he had just been told a very funny joke and took a short drink.
Then, without the smile on his lips fading, he
observed:

[

—Your eyes are not only beautiful, my child, they are also transparent. And they speak to me of something else. I've noticed how you look at Daniel. And I've also seen how he looked at you.

—It seems you want to guess everything today," said Camila, a little uncomfortably.

—Maybe I'm a bit of a witch.

—Well, that's where you're wrong," said Camila firmly, though trying not to be rude. I have told you the truth.

Mapuca took one last sip, counting the rest of the drink left in his glass. Then, running his tongue over his lips still wet with liquor, he said:

—Since you've come in here, my child, you haven't said a single word that was true.

CHAPTER 17

What are you saying? —

asked Camila,
          perplexed.

          —What I said," the Mapuche woman reaffirmed in her words. I am old enough to know that you are hiding something, although I don't know what it is.

Camila opened her mouth to answer, but Mapuca raised her hand as if begging her to let her finish.

—It doesn't matter that you lied, nor do you have to tell me what made you do it, my girl.

—The important thing is that your face does not lie, and that your body, somewhere deep down, hides a pain that prevents you from being honest. I only hope that someday you can overcome that pain and let the poison that binds you come to the surface. As long as it's in there, it can only hurt you.

Camila looked away, as if she did not dare face the woman who might be her mother, but who, in her

[

judgment, was going too far. Suddenly she noticed that one of the tea cookies was crumbled in her hand.

Perhaps, without realizing it, he had clenched his fist too hard on her. He dropped the crushed cookie on the table and shook the crumbs out of his palm.

—You know? —he said suddenly. Perhaps I am not the only one who has not told the truth here today.

Mapuca didn't say anything, but his face remained unoppressive, hieratic, and Camila seemed to read in him that look that in the card game they call poker face, which indicated to her that that comment that he had ventured a little at random, with the sole purpose of getting on the defensive, was not completely off track.

—There's only one important thing," said the Mapuche after a brief silence, "the rest of it is irrelevant at this point. And what matters is that both of us, each in our own way, love Daniel.

From that moment on, the two women remained silent, as if suddenly there were nothing more to say to each other. Or as if something inside them told them that, if they did, they could bring up things in the conversation that neither of them needed to come out. Mapuca lit another cigarette to kill time, and Camila, for her part, entertained herself by eating tea cookies. After a while, Daniel was back with the box.

—Here it is," he said, stretching out the box to Mapuca.

The woman opened it and took out the charred wooden doll. It looked like a human figure, just as she had been told. It was very schematic and represented a little man with his arms down. Mapuca did not need to look at it more than once to make his ruling.

—What I imagined," he said, "is an Anchimallén.

—What's that? —Daniel asked.

[

—An evil spirit, as opposed to a Pillan, who's a good spirit. If it were the latter, he'd have his arms up.

—And that means...?

—I think it confirms what I've told you. It's a kind of curse..., the punishment that should redeem the guilt through death... —The woman turned the figure around watching it with apprehension. The woman turned the figure over, looking at it with apprehension. The wrinkles on her face seemed to sink in as she looked at it.

—Now all that remains is for the mask to be confirmed," said Camila.

—No need," said Daniel, "I know. The two women looked at him in surprise.

—While I was downstairs Andrea called me and we talked for a while," he explained. I asked him about the mask, and he confirmed that it looked like an owl. He said it was creepy, very red in color and with evil features. The poor thing cried.

—Poor Andreita," exclaimed Mapuca sadly. So, there is no doubt that she represents the death—bird...

—There's something else," said Daniel. Andrea told me that it seems that the mask was the content of the last package, just as you had suggested. They found the box open and empty on the floor of the room from which her father jumped, which makes the investigators think that the mask was inside.

That assumption is extended to the other cases, so the rest of the suicides must have received the mask in the fifth package as well.

—The mask of the witch—bird..." Mapuca muttered, staring into the void. The witch—bird has returned to take his revenge...

Daniel felt a chill run through his body. Not because of what his nanny had just said, but because that phrase

[

reminded him so much of another he had heard not long ago, under the fiery gaze of an erupting volcano. Those words said something like the gods who seek revenge, and Camila had uttered them. She looked at this one and saw her lost too, like Mapuca, in her own thoughts. Then, addressing the Mapuche, he said:

—"You don't think it's the mask that forced those poor wretches to jump, do you?

—There are many things we don't know, my boy," the woman said, and her face once again seemed tired and discouraged, which in the eyes of her employer made her age several years in a few seconds.

—Are you saying what I think? That the mask is really possessed by that evil spirit of which you speak?

—she asked, not giving credit to what the Mapuche woman seemed to imply.

—Throughout my life, some of the nights I have been alone," said the Mapuche mournfully, "I have sensed the witch—bird flying over the earth... But that is something that only a Mapuche can understand, my boy... Then, observing him with a glazed, almost lost look, he added, "There are things in this world that are better not known...

Daniel hugged his babysitter, moved. Although all those absurd ideas seemed to him to be nothing more than fantasies, he could not help but feel a growing unease as he learned more details of the story. It seemed as if an evil being was effectively stalking him from the shadows, ready to emerge from the darkness at any moment to fulfil his destiny. He kissed the dark, worn hair of the Mapuca and held her in that position silently, allowing himself to be invaded unavoidably by the darkest thoughts. Camila looked at the motherly scene composed by his friend and that sad and intelligent woman, who seemed to keep a secret that was breaking her soul. Suddenly, an idea occurred to her, which she expressed just as it came to her mind:

—"I know a wise old Mapuche man near Pucon

—I don't know if he'll still be alive, my grandmother introduced me to him years ago. I think we could go and see him. Maybe he can give us a little more insight into this mystery.

—I'm in," said Daniel with a smile. There's not much else we can do either.

The idea of going back to Pucón with Camila seemed very appealing to him, and although he didn't trust that it would bring any new information to all that, he was sure that the journey by motorbike to the land of the volcano god would take his mind off, if only for a little while, those witch—birds and evil spirits that had invaded his imagination with dark omens.

—All you have left is that cartridge in the chamber," said Mapuca, as if he could read her thoughts.

—Do you have a better proposal? —Daniel asked cheerfully. The idea of filming with Camila again on the road had unexpectedly put him in a good mood.

—Going to the police, for example," said the woman in a tired tone. It seemed that, unlike with Daniel, she had lost the overflowing energy that animated her.

—Don't worry, he said, kissing her again. As I told you before, I don't think there's anything they can do. They're not going to put a policeman on me around the clock, and besides, I don't think that policeman was any match for the evil witch—bird," he joked, trying to cheer up his nanny.

—This is no joke, my boy," she replied sadly.

—I know, Mapu, I know," agreed Daniel, a little sorry for his frivolity, and kissed her on the head again, "but one day I have to die. And if that day is near, I don't want

[

to spend my last hours worried and surrounded by cops. If my days end here, I want to feel in my face once again the onslaught of the road air.

Mapuca did not raise his face so that no one would notice that the tears had come to his eyes again. He simply said:

—"Go then, my child.

—Are you crying? —he asked, stroking his head.

—It's nothing, Daniel, really," she answered with a smile, as she wiped away her tears. Too many emotions for one afternoon.

—Nothing will happen, you'll see," he tried to comfort her.

—I know, my boy," she agreed with a sigh. I would just like to ask you one more thing...

—Whatever," answered Daniel.

—The photos you say you received... Please keep them in a safe place. Don't you dare break them.

—I wasn't going to, he said. But why do you care?

—It may seem silly," he said, looking at Camila as well, "but some Mapuches think that images capture people's souls. When you break a picture, you are destroying the receptacle of that little piece of soul and in doing so you are endangering the person's life.

Camila and Daniel looked at Mapuca with a touch of love.

—Don't worry, Mapu, if my life depends on what happens to those photos, you can be sure they're safe —he said with a smile.

—Thank you," she said, "and forgive the nonsense of this superstitious old woman.

Camila looked at him sympathetically and thought that indeed he seemed ten years older now than when he first saw her, and thought he realized at what precise

[

moment this transformation had begun to take place. Just as she held the burned—out figure of the fearsome Anchimallén in her hands.

—Now we're going," said Daniel to Mapuca, and turning to Camila, he added: "If you don't mind, I'd like to go and see Andrea for a moment. She was a mess when I talked to her.

—Of course, go," said Camila, "and if you like, I'll see you tomorrow morning, and then we'll leave for Pucon.

Mapuca said that she would stay in the apartment for a while, finishing up everything, and said goodbye to them. As he hugged Camila, he asked her in the ear to take care of his child; and the hug she gave him seemed to go on forever. When Daniel left his house accompanied by Camila, he had the look that his old nanny had offered him when he said goodbye. In his eyes he could read clearly that she was convinced that this was the last time they would ever see each other.

Alone in the apartment, Mapuca returned to the table. Her legs were dragging her more than carrying her. She felt wilted, exhausted, as if the weight of the whole earth had suddenly fallen on her. She took her glass from the table and once again filled it with the sweet liquor. She took it to her mouth and the faint burning that invaded her breast seemed to lighten her sadness a little. He covered the bottle and put it back. He closed the door of the cabinet and walked into the house. In the kitchen, on a chair, was her bag. She opened it and took out an envelope from inside. He drank from his glass again and savored for a moment the pleasant taste that the alcohol had left in his throat. Then, pausing, he opened the envelope in his hands, took out one of the pictures in it, and looked at it for a long time. In it, as in the other photographs in the envelope, was Daniel. In the photograph he was holding at that moment he was

[

asleep on the sofa in the room where the three of them had been talking that afternoon. Next to him, on a chair, rested an old T— shirt belonging to his brother and a silver Zippo lighter.

Tears filled the eyes of the Mapuche woman and the terrible words she had uttered that same afternoon came back to her lips in a whisper:

The witch—bird has returned to take his revenge...

CHAPTER 18

The previous afternoon, a dense calima had he Chilean climate was sometimes capricious.

lazily gravitated over the city, but, after a strong night storm that unloaded on the northern half of the country, the morning rose bright and propitious for a trip. The rays of the sun had abandoned the yellowish hue that the summer heat had given them, becoming a bright white light like that of an early autumn day. The fresh air brought by the rain had cleared the atmospheric caligne and a pure and splendid sky, barely speckled by some very white cirrus that seemed to have been taken from the palette of a painter, invited, almost in a shout, to get on a motorbike and take to the road.

First thing in the morning, Camila and Daniel set off. The motorcycles rode smoothly on the asphalt, as if they were making love to him. The contact of their tyres with the road surface, like the diamond of a needle, when it cleanly traversed the grooves of an old vinyl, would rip out a beautiful melody in its wake. The infinite line of the road stretched until it was lost in a blue horizon, as if, captivated by its beauty, it tried to catch it without consequence. Daniel thought something similar was happening to him with Camila. He looked at her in front of him, cutting the air with his motorbike, and had the feeling that at any moment she would be taken by the wind and snatched up from the skies by the ancient Mapuche gods, as happened to the beautiful Ailín, who was kidnapped blindly in love by the powerful Rucapillán volcano. And he would then be like the unfortunate Tupaq, looking day after day, year after year, towards

[

the distant and terrible mountain that treasured the captive beauty of the Mapuche princess.

He noticed her aquamarine jacket waving in the wind and the Mapuche flag stitched in the middle. Why wouldn't she have told him she was of Mapuche descent? He suddenly felt a slight discomfort in the sting of his hand. It was almost healed, but it kept its tongue out because it was a little irritated by the rubbing, and although the wound usually hardly bothered him, from time to time it would prick him, as if it wanted to send him a message reminding him that a sentence was hanging over his head. He decided to concentrate on driving and on that wonderful day. Maybe he would end up losing Camila or maybe that was his last day on this earth, but if that was the case and he had to die, he thanked the sky for sending him that gift full of sunshine, pure air and a blue as intense and radiant as the one he had once seen in the changing eyes of his Mapuche princess.

They filmed for several hours and covered a large part of the journey. Daniel, perhaps as a result of those thoughts about the time he had left to live, seemed to have sharpened his perception and had become soaked in each and every sensation the route had offered him. He felt everything with more intensity, as if every stimulus from the outside world that came to his senses, rather than activating them, hit them, as if they were impacts rather than sensations. Of color, of smell, of sound. The infinite tones of the meadow, of the trees, of the hills, of the bushes; the different aromas of earth, of grass, of chlorophyll, of cattle..; the gentle rubbing of the air on his skin, the swaying of the motorbike adapting to a curve, the rumble of the engine, the cadence of the wind, the whistle of speed... He imagined the road as a metaphor for life, each kilometer travelled as a space of time that would no longer return, as if one were

[

devouring one's own existence as one moved towards the inexplicable, towards one's own destiny. And, as with life, he thought that the important thing was not where one had to go, but the path one was going to take. And he knew he was happy. That he was happy to have been able to make the road part of that vital path that had been given to him and that he felt full because he had been able to ride it on his bike. He thought that he wanted to live, that he wanted to ride thousands of kilometers more in his girl and know as many other places. But he also knew that nothing would happen if everything ended there, if the time he had been given came to an end. He had drunk the cup of life and quenched his thirst for existence, or, as his brother would have said, he had always conjugated the verb to live in the present, in the now, and he couldn't find a better way to say goodbye to life than by doing what he loved best in the world, flying in the wind over his star of the night, letting go when the road turns, and doing it with the girl with the most beautiful eyes he could ever imagine.

They stopped for lunch, as was their custom, at a roadhouse. They chatted animatedly about everything and nothing in particular. Anything that came into their heads immediately became an exciting topic of discussion or an excuse to make a joke. They talked casually, as if the dark part of life had been erased from their heads. As if there had never been any packages, pictures or masks. As if they had just met and were discovering each other at that moment. Not in a single moment did they mention the reason for their new trip to Pucon or the danger that lay ahead for Daniel. It was as if the storm of the previous day had carried away with it the pain of their lives, as if the shadows that had enveloped their relationship on the last trip had dissipated in the same way that the night fades with the

[

arrival of the dawn. They returned to the road after smoking a cigarette and getting some rest, and this time it was Daniel who led the way. His head was clear, and his thoughts followed one another like the shallow currents of a river; they hardly came to the surface, they were lost in the rushing stream of his mind. He often felt this sensation when he was rolling, as if his whole being was flowing with the road and he hardly noticed that he was driving or moving, as if everything was happening around him naturally without his intervention. It was a similar sensation to the one he had experienced

The first time he practiced meditation, as a kind of state of grace in which his being merged with the world and this and that ceased to be two different things, to become one and the same entity.

The hours passed, the stages followed one another, and the day and the road were left behind. It occurred to Daniel that he and Camila were like two wandering stars in an immutable orbit that led them irretrievably back to Pucon, and that that road was as beautiful and inexorable to them as the elliptical path that the sun draws repeatedly in its endless wandering through space. He thought then that perhaps it was there that he would receive the fifth package with the mask of the witch—bird. He would not be surprised, because the previous one had been delivered in Argentina. If that was so, perhaps that was the place where he was going to die, by Lake Villarrica, under the conical gaze of the volcano. He didn't think it was a bad place to leave this life, and although that thought was somewhat somber, he couldn't help but have a sad smile on his face. They had arrived in Pucón.

They took the same hotel as last time, also with separate beds, and they went out for a walk before dinner. The next day, they would meet the old Mapuche

[

man who might be able to shed some light on that mystery. That time was a little earlier than the last one, but even so, the sun was retreating, throwing soft orange rays that melancholically lengthened the shadows cast by the city. Daniel contemplated the peaceful light that rested on Camila like an infinity of golden butterflies, and thought that the clarity of Pucon suited him well, as if, admiring her beauty, he wanted to embrace her and wrap her in a soft luminous caress. The afternoon air, charged with the smell of the nearby woods, oxygenated the peaceful streets—quotes, bathing them with a benign freshness. After a pleasant walk, they had dinner in the same place as last time, and as if they missed that time and wanted to repeat it, they went to the bar where they had been talking and having drinks with the group of young bikers. This time they also had Jägermeister with Red Bull, but in a more moderate way, just for champagne. Then, before returning to the hotel, they decided to go and see the volcano in front of the lake of Villarrica. Daniel cherished for a few moments the idea that perhaps, if everything was happening more or less the same way, the kiss they gave each other would be repeated too. But he quickly put that idea out of his mind. Camila had made it clear to him when they were in Argentina that this would not happen again and he did not want to let frustration embitters his day, which could almost be described as perfect. They arrived in front of the lake and found it just as lonely and beautiful as the last time. It was no longer full moon and an immaculate waning moon shone on the cone of the volcano, as if a mischievous little devil, confusing the satellite with a cheese, had taken a bite out of it, leaving only a white and lonely piece. In spite of that, or perhaps because the moonlight was less and did not overshadow them, the stars shone even brighter this time, and seemed much

[

more numerous, as if the firmament had summoned them to come and illuminate the sad biker's last night.

—Do you know that in the northern hemisphere you can see the stars upside down? —asked Daniel, gazing in wonder at the Southern Cross.

—Yes," replied Camila, looking out over the cosmos as well. Remember that I am a Mapuche. I'm sure I can teach you a lot of things about the sky that you don't know, city boy.

Daniel looked at the girl's face, illuminated by the blue light of the moon, and felt a crazy desire to kiss her. But instead of doing so, he said to her with a discouraging smile:

—Oh, yeah? —Like what, for instance?

—The moon," she said. "What phase is it in?

—He said, "A tongue—in—cheek. My brother taught me a little trick as a child. Whenever you see it in the shape of a C, it's in a crescent. And if the phase is decreasing, you can see it as a D.

—That's only half true," she said with a smile. In the northern hemisphere the opposite is true.

—It's okay," he admitted. One by one. What else can you tell me?

—Do you see that cluster of stars near the constellation of Orion? —No.

—You mean the Pleiades?

—Yes," she confirmed, "when I was a child my grandmother Aimara used to tell me that the stars were the souls of the dead who ascended to heaven and became messengers of the gods. Their function was to visit us every night to bring us hope in the midst of darkness and to remind us humans that, although day after day blackness swallows up the sun and envelops

[
161]

the Earth, the light has not been extinguished, but continues to exist somewhere

—And what about the Pleiades? —he asked.

—My grandmother said that this group of stars were the ancestors of our tribe..." Camila turned her eyes away from the sky and looked at Daniel with a sad look that had taken on a delicate shade of turquoise. I always thought that story about the permanence of light conveyed hope...

—Thank you," he said.

—For what? —she asked.

—I know you told me that beautiful story for that... —to give me hope...

Camila looked at the sky again without answering and it seemed to Daniel that his eyes had become wet.

—I believe that when your soul goes up to heaven, it won't join the Pleiades," he said, looking at her. He will kick Sirius away and put himself in his place.

—And why do you think that? —I want to know.

—Because Sirius is the most luminous star in the observable firmament, and that place can only be yours.

Daniel didn't care at all how corny those words might have sounded; he just said them as he felt them and, once said, he didn't regret it. He felt naughty, free. The Jägermeister was having its effect and a very pleasant tingling had settled on his chest. Camila looked at him with a reproachful expression on her face, but when she was about to reproach him for going that way, he, as he had done on another occasion, placed his index finger gently on her lips and said

—What do you care if I compliment you? Soon, when I get the fifth package, I won't be able to do it anymore. Let me explain now that I can still...

—Don't say such things even as a joke," she protested, "I'm looking at the volcano now. Then, after a few seconds of silence, she added, "Do you think Ailin is still in there?

—No," he replied, pulling his hair away from her so that he could see her face better. I didn't know that, but now I know that the Mapuche princess has long since been a prisoner.

—Where is she then? —Camila asked.

—Right now, she's here, next to me...

The girl looked at him in a daze and hesitated for a few moments, then, gently removing her hand from his face, she said:

—I think we'd better get back to the hotel.

—I think we'd better get back to the hotel. —I'm not leaving here without taking a bath, it might be the last one I can enjoy!

—Don't keep saying things like that! —She scolded him.

—Are you in? —asked Daniel, as he stripped to his underwear.

—No," she said, uncomfortable at his nakedness.

I'd rather wait for you here.

Daniel looked into her eyes and seemed to find in them, just as he had in the hotel in Mendoza, a glimmer of desire.

—You're missing it," he said with a mischievous smile, and plunged into the clear waters of Lake Villarrica.

Camila leaned on a huge araucaria tree and watched Daniel. He was splashing around and screaming like a child in the water, and the girl laughed heartily at him having fun like that. Even though it was a great night, no one else was seen on the lake, and it didn't take her long

[

to feel the urge to join him. Without thinking too much about it, she stayed in her underwear and went into the water as well. When Daniel saw her, he ran to her and splashed her laughing like the other time. She splashed him in revenge, and the two of them engaged in a small battle in which they ended up struggling to see who could get the other's head underwater. Daniel picked up Camila in the air and threw her forward, bamboozling her into the lake. She got up laughing, and he thought he was watching a Mapuche goddess emerge from the waters. The drops slipped gently on her shoulders as when she came out of the shower at the hotel, but now she was even more beautiful, so much so that she eclipsed the very beauty of the stars. The wet fabric of the bra fitted her breasts like a second skin and the coolness of the water made the nipples stand out like two little cherries, which Daniel found as dangerous as two sharp daggers pointing at his heart. He was paralyzed by the feeling that his body was burning up under the water at the sight of that overwhelming vision. She lunged at him, screaming:

—Now you will see!

Daniel held her by the arms and stopped her body at a minimum distance from his. He stared at her full of desire, but saw that in her eyes fear had suddenly appeared. He let go of her wrists and took her gently by the hands. He could hardly resist the urge to pounce on her and fill her with kisses, but those fearful eyes made him sad. What was he afraid of? Then he realized that the fear he read in her eyes was different from what he had seen on other occasions. Now he was sure that Camila was afraid of herself, of her own desire. He felt her suddenly tremble in his arms and continued to look at her without daring to take a step forward, but without daring to let go of her either, because he was sure that

[

if he did that, he would never hold her so close again. The two looked at each other without being able to look away from each other, as if hypnotized, while a stream of desire ran through their drenched bodies. He gently stroked her fingertips with his fingers, and felt as if that light, barely perceptible contact gave him a high—voltage electric shock, which he could hardly bear. His sex hardened more and more under water, and he felt her blood like an overflowing torrent responding to the silent call of the body in front of him. Finally, Camila, in a pleasing whisper, barely audible on that starry night, said:

—This is crazy, Daniel... —You have to understand that it gives maybe whatever I want... I mustn't... I can never kiss

you... So, he, ignoring those absurd words and

incomprehensible, ignoring all the pain that accompanied them and which they were capable of provoking, did something completely unexpected: he smiled.

—Why are you smiling? —she asked, perplexed.

And he, without letting the smile escape his lips, answered:

—Because every time you tell me that, I know you're going to kiss me. She looked at Daniel in astonishment for a few moments and looked at that untimely smile. Then, without knowing why she was doing it, ignoring her own will and all the voices screaming inside her, which were desperately demanding that she run away, she answered:

—You're right.

Then she put her lips to his smile and kissed it. Daniel felt his whole being electrified by the contact of those lips, pressed the girl against him and put his tongue in

[

her mouth. Camila responded with her own tongue and he felt again the sweet taste of the saliva and breath of his Mapuche princess, wet and burning. With the thirsty man's desire and urgency, but without stopping kissing her, he stripped her of her bra, and then, his tongue left hers to slide, through her neck, to her breasts. She responded to his contact with a groan, which sounded in the night like that of a beautiful animal whose life had slipped away. Daniel lifted her into the air and as his tongue ran hungry across her sweet nipples, his fingers ventured into the secret, dark realms between her thighs. Camila, ecstatic, squirmed with pleasure in Daniel's arms, abandoning herself to his caresses and letting him release all the desire he had been accumulating for so long. Then she clung to him like a hungry wolf, and she too tasted the virile fruits of his body, making him tremble at the advance of his mouth. Daniel felt dragged by pleasure, as if he were a child lost in a hurricane, he looked up at the sky, at the stars, and they disappeared, and with them, the lake, the volcano, the moon, the whole world. Only he and she remained, as if the rest of the universe were hiding so as not to hinder the reunion, after so many years of waiting, of the Mapuche chief Tupaq and his Mapuche princess. Kissing again and again, as if they both thought it was the last one they were going to do, their bodies gave themselves repeatedly to the game of love. He entered her and it seemed as if, as their bodies joined together, so did their souls, and after having waited so long, he thought with tears in his eyes that if there was a perfect day for it to be the last, there could be no better one.

When their bodies spilled all their desire, the two bikers, exhausted and sweaty, but unable to move away from each other, lay on the shore, next to the beautiful araucaria tree. Daniel felt calm, invaded by an enormous

[

calm like he hadn't felt in a long, long time. Camila embraced him and gently caressed the tree of life on his back, as if with her caresses she wished to divert the primordial sap from its trunk and branches and breathe it into his veins, so that it would run through them, vivifying him and drawing him away from death. Daniel, in turn, kissed the tattoo on her shoulder, the Mapuche symbol of the eyes that can see the soul.

—Why now? —he asked suddenly.

Those were the first words spoken after their bodies stopped talking. He had uttered them without really knowing why, convinced that she would not answer them. He looked into her eyes and thought they were even more beautiful after making love. But sadness was still in them, now, perhaps even more than before. Indeed, Camila did not answer. She turned her gaze to the imposing mountain of Rucapillán, which she had watched silently as they made love, and remained silent. Daniel didn't insist, he remained embraced by her, feeling the soft beat of his heart through his skin, and he too looked at the volcanic giant. Suddenly, a slightly foolish idea came into his head.

—If anything, ever happens to me," he said, "I mean... if I die, I will protect you wherever I am... I promise...

—You're not going to die," she denied, without looking at him. Don't say such things.

—I just wanted you to know," he said, kissing her tenderly on the head.

He felt at peace with himself, and it seemed that nothing could break that feeling, but unexpectedly a disturbing thought came out of all the quietness that ran through his body. Perhaps it was the image of the silent volcano under the stars that brought him. He knew it was an absurd idea, but still he could not help but shudder at the thought. It occurred to him that Ruca— Piptan had

[

been watching them as they made love, and unlike the last time, she had not unleashed her fury of lava and fire. And he realized that now that he had been with her, he no longer wanted to die. He knew that what had happened that night at the lake had grabbed him desperately, and he suddenly felt the fear of death come over him again. But there was something that frightened him even more, something that he knew was impossible to happen, but that he could not help thinking about. The idea that Rucapillán was waiting to take his Mapuche princess away from him, that, inside his rocky bowels, hatred and jealousy were preparing a terrible deflagration, and that that very night, the mountain god would come for Camila, without anything or anyone being able to prevent it. He embraced her tightly, and whispered softly in her ear two words that she would never have thought she would utter that day: "I love you.

Her beautiful eyes looked at him, and he discovered that they had been filled with tears, but they were also full of fear. He then looked over his head at the mountain, afraid that Rucapillán might have heard him. From the dark volcano nothing came to him but his silent stare of stone, and Daniel thought that he would have preferred a terrible eruption like the one the other day to that dumb and sinister calm, and to that silence full of threats.

CHAPTER 19

U the brightness that the new day brought. In nder her closed eyelids, her pupils perceived his head, still a little lethargic from sleep, floated like a distant chimera the image of Camila naked embracing him. He opened his eyes and saw that it had not been a dream, and thought that, if it had been, it had crossed the unconscious world of fantasy to become reality. Next to him, in the same bed, in which there was barely room for both of them, slept his Mapuche princess wrapped in a swirl of curly hair. Above her, on the other side of the room, he could see the other bed unmade. In the dim morning light, the sleeping girl looked like a gift from the gods, and Daniel felt his chest brimming with happiness. Another day and he was still alive. More alive than ever, in fact. He stood still, looking at the woman sleeping next to him, as if he didn't believe she was there, almost afraid to close his eyes in case it was just a mirage that was going to fade away just before I opened them again. He thought that was what he wanted to see for the rest of his life when he woke up, every morning of every month of every year... Then he realized that maybe there would be no more years, no more months, and an inopportune thought brought him the image of the volcano. He made an effort to put that gloomy vision out of his mind. Maybe the old Mapuche man he was going to meet today could provide him with information that would help him conjure up the danger, put that threat away forever before the nightmare in the shape of a bird mask became a reality.

—I know you're looking at me," said Camila's adoring voice, "but I haven't opened my eyes yet.

[

—Mmm..." Daniel muttered, stretching his limbs a little and not afraid to wake her up. And how do you know?

Some Mapuche trick?

She opened her eyes and to him it seemed as if two windows to the sky were opening.

—I just had a feeling," she replied dully, with a beautiful smile that seemed to have been painted on her face by God himself.

Daniel pulled his hair out of her face gently. He had gotten used to doing that and loved it. He thought that this girl had brought back feelings that had been buried for a long time. It was as if his senses went back to the past and he felt life again with the strength and intensity of a teenager. He looked at Camila and it seemed to him that he was looking at a woman for the first time, as if in her body, in her gestures, in her voice, he was discovering life again, as if he had never loved anyone else before. He approached her slowly and gently kissed her lips. She embraced herself to him and locked his legs with hers, as if he feared she would escape. Daniel needed no more for his body to respond as if someone had pressed a switch that transmitted a magical current into his body.

—Don't go too far," she stopped him, but without much conviction. ... Look at the time before, we're meeting at eleven...

—I can't stop," he protested, caressing her and kissing her neck. I'm not my own master anymore... I'm just a puppet.

—What is this nonsense? —She laughed without leaving him.

—That you've bewitched me with your Mapuche spells, and my hands only do what you want, so you're the only one to blame. —He raised one hand pretending to have it out of control and tried to hold it with the other hand, as if he were trying with all his strength without being able to stop it from going to her chest. See? I can't do anything!

—Clown! —she laughed, kissing him and pressing her body against his.

They made love and then, a little hastily, for it was late, they took a shower and left the room. They went to Berlin, an elegant and cozy café, where they had arranged to meet Aukan, the Mapuche sage known to Camila. They were relieved to see that he had not yet arrived; they would not have liked to keep him waiting, because, according to Camila, it could be considered disrespectful. They ordered some coffee with milk served in bowls in the Berlin style and, on the waiter's recommendation, some delicious sprit— zkuchen to go with it.

It did not take long for old Aukan to arrive. Daniel calculated that he could be about seventy—five or eighty years old, although he seemed to retain an energy and vigour unbecoming his age. He had angular but distinguished features, black hair barely visited by grey hair, and a multitude of wrinkles furrowed his sun— tanned face. Before Camila told him it was him, Daniel had recognized him by his clothes. He wore a traditional Mapuche poncho and a headband tied to his forehead, and he supported the weight of his body, slightly bent over the years, on a carved wooden stick, whose handle was shaped like a lizard or a snake. The only discordant element with the attire was a fretworked panama hat in a cream tone in the Western style. Daniel felt that its delicate and ceremonious gestures gave it an aura of authority. Both bikers got up as soon as they saw him enter and Camila greeted him friendly, but with

[

deference, even with a certain reverential fear. The Indian looked curiously at Daniel with his gray, watery eyes. To him they seemed as old as the world itself, but, although they were worn out from so much looking over the years, they retained their brightness and vivacity.

That almost supernatural look reminded him of something biker, but I didn't know exactly what.

—Thank you for agreeing to see us," said Daniel by way of greeting.

—It would have been rude not to," the old man replied with a smile as he took his seat in front of them. Especially when the request comes from Aimara's granddaughter.

—I thank you, Lonco," said Camila, smiling back at him, though he could not conceal the discomfort he felt about his family.

—Lonco? —Daniel wondered.

—Lonco is the name given to the head of a Mapuche tribe or clan," she explained.

—I'm just a poor old man with a disease," said Aukan, playing down the title as he gently stroked the handle of his stick with the thin phalanges that had been somewhat deformed by the arthritis. The age of the great leaders of our people is lost in the distant mists of time. —Then he looked at Daniel with his kind eyes and said, "Tell me, what has brought you to me?

Camila and Daniel explained the story in detail to the Mapuche, and he listened carefully to everything they had to say. When they finished, the man reflected for a few moments and then said

—"I think your Mapuche friend is right. I couldn't say for sure, because there are many traditions of our people and not all of them have a univocal interpretation, but

[

173]

from what they tell me, everything points to the fact that the witch—bird will visit you soon, boy. I am truly sorry.

—But why me? —asked Daniel, as he felt his skin crawl when he heard the name of that evil character. I haven't done anything...

—As I was told your friend told you, it may have something to do with your company... —the old man speculated. Five boxes, five companies, five partners.

—But I have nothing to do with my company," Daniel despaired. I want to say that I have not participated in any of its activities... It is managed by professionals who are accountable to a board of directors...

—Do you mean the shepherd is not responsible for what his sheep do?

Daniel stared in amazement at the old Mapuche. He couldn't believe he was justifying accusing him of something he hadn't done. He felt a wave of anger coming over him.

—I never thought I'd say this," he replied heatedly.

But it seems to me that the Mapuche people are unfair.

Camila squeezed Daniel's hand tightly, as if to urge him to shut up, but he looked at her shaking his head and then looked at the Mapuche again.

—No. —That's not fair. It's me they want to kill. At least I'll say what I think.

—Please, Lonco, don't listen to my friend," begged Camila to the old man. Fear and despair speak from his mouth...

—No, Camila, the boy is right," said Aukan slowly. He's the one who's going to die. At least he should be allowed to speak.

—Why do you say I'm going to die? —asked Daniel with increasing excitement. That remains to be seen.

[

The Mapuche chief looked at him sadly.

—If it is true that the witch—bird is after you," he said ruefully, "then history has already been written.

—Well, I'll rewrite it! —shouted the biker, getting up and making a sudden move.

—Daniel! —exclaimed Camila, frightened.

He turned to her and discovered a silent plea in her beautiful eyes. Then he realized that his nerves had betrayed him and that neither she nor that poor old man were his enemies. He felt ashamed and sat down again. He was trembling.

—I beg your forgiveness, Aukan," he said, feeling his anger turn to sadness. It is not your fault, and I have disrespected you when you have come here to do me a favor... I do not know what has happened to me...

—What's wrong with you is what you'd expect to happen to anyone who is threatened with death," the Mapuche replied sweetly, as he placed his gnarled hand on Daniel's. You are confused and angry... Sometimes we rebel against our destiny instead of assuming it, and that is painful.

—I understand what you're saying, Aukan," said Daniel more calmly, "but I'm not going to accept that I'm going to die just like that.

—Whatever will happen will happen," said the old man, "I can only tell you that if you really are under the gaze of the witch—bird, there is not much you can do. The Gods are demanding reparation, and they have fixed the amount of reparation at five souls. Not one more, not one less.

—But that's not fair," Daniel repeated.

—Justice is something that everyone imagines in their head in a different way," said Aukan, "and no one sees it the same way. We all think it should favor us, when, in

[

fact, it should favor no one, because favor is something done to one person to the detriment of another.

—But I can't be held responsible for acts I haven't committed," insisted Daniel, as he nervously turned his bowl over the plate.

—That's not how the Mapuche gods see it," the old chief objected.

—I don't want to offend you, Aukan," said Daniel, trying to choose his words so as not to offend the old man, for whom Camila seemed to have a deep respect, "but his culture is different from the West. Our criminal laws require to punish a person who is responsible, and they associate that responsibility with an act. And that is a fundamental part of what we consider civilization.

The Mapuche's compassionate eyes twinkled like a burning ember when they heard those words, and his face was transformed for a moment into that of an avenging god. Then Daniel knew what that gray look of the old man reminded him of: the eyes of a wolf. He had the impression that he had gone too far, and was about to apologize when he saw that after a few moments the old man's gaze had returned to its peaceful and calm appearance.

—Civilization? —asked the old man with a sad smile. Indeed, our concepts of many things differ from you. Before the Westerners arrived with their civilization, our lands were blankets of greenery which we shared with the animals, and all of us, the trees, the beasts and the men, felt like brothers, sons of the earth.

Daniel remained silent. He realized that the man was very inward looking and didn't really stick to his arguments for progress, and in fact he wasn't very clear about what you could call progress and what you couldn't. He loved nature as much as he did, and he had

[

always thought that technological advances had to be carefully combined with nature.

—About fifteen or twenty years ago," the Mapuche continued, "the forests around Pucón and all over the Araucanía were even greener and more luxuriant. But a series of arson fires with a clear economic purpose devastated several hectares, devastating the natural heritage of our ancestors. Thousands of animals and plants were devoured by the fire of that which you call civilization... It even took some human lives... —The grey look of the Indian seemed lost somewhere in the story he was telling, as if he himself was contemplating at that very moment the flames, the death and the devastation. It has taken many years to reforest part of that desert and it will never be the same again. But no one has paid for that. Those criminal laws you speak of have not put those responsible in jail. Is that civilization?

—No... of course not, —replied Daniel a little confused. —But just because our laws don't always work, doesn't mean they aren't fair...

—I'll tell you a story, if you allow me," said the Mapuche. Daniel nodded his head and the Indian chief began his narration.

—Many thousands of years ago, the sun—god created the first Mapuches and left them to their fate on the barren surface of the earth. As they had nothing to eat, they were hungry and Kuyén, the moon goddess, took pity on them, so she took a piece of her own skin and spread it over the barren ground, immediately transforming it into a villainous orchard. Then he offered it to the humans, and told them that they could make use of it according to their needs. The men and women then took from the forests what they needed and lived in harmony with nature for a time. But one fateful day, a

[

man named Hueicha, which means war, took more than he needed and hoarded a large quantity of skins, for which he needed to kill many animals, and built himself a huge palace with hundreds of tree trunks which he had to cut down, leaving the forest bare. And although at enormous cost, he became a very rich man. After a while, he had a son whom he called Alhué, which means 'lost soul'.

Years after the death of his father, Alhué received a strange visit. One day he was in his palace enjoying his wealth when an old woman came up to him and said her name was Sayen, which means woman of great heart. When asked the reason for her visit, Sayen replied that she had come from a long journey and was tired, so she thought that in that opulent place where goods abounded, they would allow her to rest for a while and offer her some shade and some water and food to recover from the fatigue of the journey. Alhué told him that he would like to be able to offer him those things he needed, but that he could not, because a minimal sense of justice prevented him from doing so. Sayen asked, intrigued, what kind of justice is it that denies water and bread to those who need it? Alhué answered with another question:

What do you think it is to deserve? The old woman thought for a few seconds and then answered: to deserve is to reap what you have planted, that is, to receive something according to your actions. Exactly, agreed Alhué. So, since you have not done anything for me to give you water or food, it would be an injustice for me to do so. Sayen, after reflecting for a few moments on the words of Hueicha's son, asked him: "No... it's true that it was your father who built all this..." "That's right", replied Alhué in surprise. "According to that, said the old woman, you shouldn't be the one to enjoy it, since you

[

have done nothing to possess it". Alhué was perplexed by this argument, but quickly added: "We, the children, are heirs of our parents, and therefore we deserve to receive the fruits of their actions, even if we have not participated in them".

The old woman then removed the cloak that covered her arm and showed the Mapuche a wound that pierced it from side to side. The yaga oozed pus and was full of worms, and from it emanated a horrible stench of putrefaction. Alhué was horrified to see it and sent his servants to throw out of his palace that old woman who had come to deprive him of his happiness by showing him the ugliness of her body. When the servants were going to obey, a marvelous white light flooded the room in which they were and the old woman showed her true nature transforming herself into Kuyen, the Goddess—Moon. Alhué turned away terrified and begged not to hurt her. Kuyen approached him and told him that she only wanted to be fair with him and give him what he deserved. She showed him her snowy arm and in the beauty of her young body the terrible wound remained open. "This," said the goddess moon, "is the place where my skin was, which I gladly gave to the Mapuches so that they could make use of it according to their needs. But your father took much more than he needed, and that is why my wound has rotted and I suffer continuous unbearable pain. To restore order to things, I must return this palace to the forest and punish you with death. "But why," cried the son of Hueicha in fear, "if I have done nothing to you. "Indeed," accepted Kuyen.

"But you are your father's heir and, as you have said, the children deserve to receive the fruits of their fathers' actions, even if they have not taken part in them, is it not so? Alhué opened his mouth to answer, but he could not find any word that could speak in his favor, for indeed he

[

179]

realized that if, as he had said, he could take the good that his father had achieved by his own actions, in which he had not taken part, he should also answer for his father's bad deeds, even if he had not taken part in them. At the very moment he realized this, the white light of the moon—goddess became much more intense and its luminosity destroyed the palace and Hueicha's own son, who burst out with all his wealth into thousands of tiny dust particles, which were blown by the wind into the forest, from where they should never have come. The wound on Kuyen's arm healed instantly and the balance of nature, as well as justice, was restored.

The old man Lonco finished his story and looked with his beautiful wolfish eyes at the biker, but this one, like the Indian Alhué of the story, found nothing to say.

Then, three people entered the place, which was very familiar to Daniel, but which he took a few seconds to recognize. They were the three bikers who accompanied Camila the day he met her in the bar on the road. When he realized this, he turned to his friend to make her notice, but he saw that she had changed her face and looked at them with a terrified expression. Strangely, he turned his gaze to them and saw the one they had called the Cholo step forward to the other two and approach the table they were at with a vulture's smile on his face. He was surprised that he was next to Oscar, the Mapuche motorcyclist, and Tomás, the youngest of the three, since Camila had told him that they did not know him at all and that, if he was sitting with them that day, it was only because he had been invited to do so out of courtesy to the motorcyclist.

When the Cholo arrived where they were, he gave Aukan a respectful nod.

—I salute you, Lonco," he said deferentially to the boss.

[

He responded with another nod. Daniel didn't understand anything. What could those men have known about? Then the Cholo smiled again with a sneer under his unpleasant moustache and, looking at the beautiful motorbike girl, who seemed petrified with fear, said:

—What's wrong, Camila? —Are you not going to say hello to your boyfriend?

CHAPTER 20

A guy meant by your boyfriend, but, seeing the t first, Daniel didn't quite understand what the look of desolation on Camila's face, he started to make sense of it. Was he implying they were dating? He looked at her in confusion, although at no point did it occur to him that it might be true.

—Camila? —he said.

—Daniel..." she replied with a voice, "it's not what you think... Those unoriginal words had a clear meaning for anyone who had ever heard them. But it wasn't the words themselves that were telling her something, Camila could have chosen any other, but the effect would have been the same, because it was her face that was speaking. Everything about him expressed much more clearly than his words that this guy wasn't lying, and Daniel was speechless. He didn't dare to verbalize his fears, to ask him to explain himself. He just didn't want to hear what she had to say, he didn't want her to confirm what he already knew, because that confirmation would be the hardest blow that anyone could give him at that moment.

Nevertheless, Camila spoke out:

—I should have told you," she said, barely holding back her tears, "but I didn't get the chance. I went out with him a couple of times, that's all... But it was before I met you...

Daniel couldn't believe what he was hearing. Of all the things he had heard in the last few days, and they had been many and very strange, none had seemed so absurd to him or hurt so much as that one. How was it possible that...?

[

He shook his head negatively, as if he did not quite understand what they were saying, and got up from the table.

—Please wait..." Camila pleaded.

—I have nothing more to say to you," he replied, getting ready to leave as soon as possible.

As he passed the Cholo, he let go with a snake—like smile:

—Kiss my girlfriend well, eh?

When Daniel heard that, he felt the blood boil in his veins and turned towards him, punching him in the face and making him fall to the ground.

—Daniel! —shouted Camila, frightened.

He stared at the Cholo with his clenched fists. He stood up to strike back, and as the two men lunged at each other, Aukan's wooden stick came between them with a sharp blow to the floor. Somehow, both sides felt that was an undeniable command. Daniel looked into the Mapuche's grey wolf's eyes, which silently and unmistakably demanded that it stop. Then he looked at the Cholo in anger, but he seemed to have stopped his intentions, as if Aukan's gesture was a sentence for him. Daniel took a deep breath to calm down and decided to leave. But he knew, simply by seeing the Cholo's angry look, that he had made an enemy for life. His words immediately confirmed that impression.

—You don't know what you've done, biker," he said, wiping the back of his hand over a small stream of blood that had flowed from his mouth as a result of the punch he had received. Without saying goodbye, Daniel turned around and left the premises. He ran to the hotel, possessed by rage. He could hardly breathe, and his mind was bombarded by a succession of images showing Camila and the Cholo together. He couldn't

[

resist. He couldn't understand it. He didn't even think of going up to the room to get his things, he had to get out of there as soon as possible. As he was getting on his motorbike, he saw Camila running up to him with her face waterlogged in tears.

—Daniel, please, I'm just asking you to listen to me! —she pleaded when she got to where she was.

—I don't need to hear anything to know what happened. —Or are you going to tell me that my eyes have deceived me? —he roared, trying not to burst into tears himself, as he started his motorcycle.

—I told you," she said without daring to touch him, "I didn't know you. We've only been out a couple of times... but it doesn't mean anything to me...

—You said that already," he replied shakily, with a look that frightened the girl.

—I didn't know you," she repeated. Just because I didn't tell you about my past doesn't mean I didn't have one...

Daniel looked at her, and his eyes full of fire were suddenly filled with deep sadness.

—It's not that," he said.

—Then what is it?

—It's about you are telling me you don't know him. It's about you lying to me all this time.

Her opaline eyes remained looking at him, full of tears and helpless, but her mouth did not know what to say. Daniel looked at them and realized that the pain made them even more beautiful, that even in a moment like that they possessed a special tonality.

—You lied to me, Camila. That's all it is, nothing else," he repeated as he felt his heart break at the mention of her name. He put the power to the handlebars and

[

without saying another word the bike started leaving behind a thick dust.

Camila, full of pain, saw it disappear when she turned into an intersection at the end of the street.
Something inside her told her that she would never see him again.

CHAPTER 21

T a tremendous pain stirring inside him as if a he journey back became hell for Daniel. He felt hungry animal were devouring his entrails. He wouldn't have rolled more than twenty or thirty kilometers when he had to stop in the ditch, because he felt his strength was running out. He got off the bike and took off his helmet so that he could breathe, raised his head to the sky, and screamed in pain. Then he broke into an inconsolable cry, as he had not cried for many years, as if he had been holding all those tears to release them that day in that place. A couple of bikers stopped at the side of the road to see if he needed anything, and he thanked them and said he was fine. Not quite convinced, they started back up. It was obvious that something was wrong with him, but they didn't want to get in the way. Daniel felt ashamed that they had seen him in that state. He got back on his motorbike and went back on the road. The day seemed to have blended with his mood, and the sky began to gather black clouds that wrapped the road in the horizon, as if a suffering god oozed his wound onto the earth. Daniel prayed that it wouldn't rain, he had to get to Santiago as soon as possible, he needed to put some land between him and Camila, and he didn't care that it wouldn't change anything, he just wanted to get away, even though, deep down, he knew that even if he took a plane and went to the other side of the world, he would take the pain with him.

Fortunately, the sky resisted unloading its rain, although it also captured the sun's rays with its clouds, sowing darkness all along the way. That same darkness was what he felt inside.

[

Blackness, pain and emptiness. Not even riding his motorcycle brought him comfort, because, unlike other times when he felt bad, the road served as a balm, now it was precisely the same medicine that poisoned him. The air, the asphalt, the grass, the electric poles, the cars, the motorcycles, the cows... Everything that the road brought to him reminded him of Camila and became unbearable. She began to accelerate and, without realizing it, the engine revolutions increased dangerously until exceeding the permitted speed. When he noticed this, his heart began to beat strongly and for a moment it crossed his mind to continue accelerating. He remembered his mother and brother. Then came the image of eyes as blue as the waters of Korea and as beautiful as the night. It seemed that life was trying to take away everything he wanted. Why didn't he save the witch—bird the trouble? Wasn't he supposed to kill himself anyway? Wouldn't it be better to die there, on his Midnight, than to be crushed on a sidewalk when he fell off a building? No, he was not going to die now, nor was he going to let the warlock push him into the abyss. He would face him and face his pain, too. He took a deep breath and began to decelerate, and little by little, his shoulders, his neck and his arms began to relax, as the pressure that the speed was exerting on them eased. A little later he saw a service area and decided to stop for a break. When he got off the bike, he realized that it was the same one he and Camila had been on when they came back from Pucón together. He hadn't noticed it before because it was pouring with rain that time. He was about to get back on his Midnight and get out of there, but something pushed him to get in, and not only that, it led him to choose the same table where they had both sat last time, next to a huge window that did not allow them to see anything because of the thick mantle of rain. This time he could see the landscape, and it seemed to him as dark and desolate as his soul. He breathed heavily in the greasy air that floated in the room, as if the familiar smell brought him back to happier times, and he pulled the packet of cigarettes out of his jacket pocket to light a cigarette. Together with the pack he also took a picture inadvertently. It was one of those taken while he was sleeping.

He had kept it away from the others and kept it for himself because he liked it. There he was in bed, bare—chested and half—covered by the sheet, probably after a night of partying, because the day seemed quite advanced judging by the brightness coming through the window. Or maybe he was just taking a nap. Whatever it was, he was seen in harmony, in a peaceful sleep, as if nothing in this world disturbed him. That was why he had chosen it, for that sense of peace he so badly needed. Next to him, he was resting on a chair, next to a pair of underpants and trousers that he had put on anyway, his brother's T— shirt. The Zippo was also in the picture, although it was barely visible. The snapshot showed the glow that a ray of sunshine had painted on it. He thought he missed Benjamin very much and, as if that thought had awakened the spider's poison that lay crouched in his hand, he felt a sting in his wound. He left the photograph on the table and looked down at the back of his hand cursing. It had been almost painless for some time, and now, out of the blue, the pain was coming back. Then he saw that the wound had opened up a little, probably as a result of the blow he had given that imbecile in the bar in Pucon. Although he was not left— handed, because of the position he was in next to him, that was the hand he had used to hit him. The memory of the Cholo on the floor with his mouth split encouraged him a little; it had been worth it, even though

[

188]

his wound hurt now. He lit his cigar as a young and rather attractive waitress brought him a Coca— Cola and some steaming sausages on a tray, accompanied by some onion rings. The girl smiled as she placed the tray on the table and left. Daniel hardly looked at her. He seasoned everything with a little mustard, cut the sausages into small pieces and tried one of the onion rings, but, as it was very hot, he preferred to give it time to cool down a little and finish smoking the cigar before starting to eat. He looked outside again, which was still dark and gloomy. He didn't like the view and looked away dejectedly at the onion rings that were lying on his plate.

I would have preferred it to rain and thunder, like when he was there with Camila. He remembered that she had told him that his mother told him that thunder was the voice from heaven scolding men for their bad deeds. His eyes smoked, and he felt as if a fist were clenched in his chest, oppressing his heart. He took a deep puff on his cigarette and turned his eyes outward. A zenithly sky fell languidly over the road, not quite making up its mind to throw some of the water that gave it that sad, leaden color. Camila's distressed look came to her mind when she told her about her mother. That girl seemed to have many secrets. But it didn't matter, she was no longer in his life, and she would never be again. She blew out the tobacco smoke on the window pane, and it spread over her surface like a fog over the waters of a lake. When the smoke dispersed, he could see a dog sitting outside a few feet away. Actually, it looked more like a wolf than a dog. He was looking at it with sad eyes, which reminded him of the old Mapuche. He imagined that he had been transformed into that beautiful animal and that it had been following him since Pucón. But why? To warn him of some danger? To remind him that whatever he did, he could not escape? He looked again at the food

[

on his plate and, to distract himself, he arranged with his knife and fork the onion rings and the pieces of sausage smeared with mustard so that they drew a face. Then he felt the hair on the back of his neck stand up as he realized that the resulting image looked very much like that of a terrible bird of vengeance. Quickly he tore up the picture. Everything around him seemed to be ganging up on him, every object, every image, every person seemed to come from a fantastic tale, more like a nightmare, as if the fearsome characters who populated it had escaped from its pages in the form of spectral shadows to haunt and torment him. The wolf, the bird, the volcano... He thought of that evil volcano, the jealous Rucapillán, and the hateful face of the Cholo came to his mind. He was the Rucapillán who had kidnapped Princess Ailín. The princess was Camila. And the wolf that followed him was the Mapuche chief. But who was the witch—bird then? He looked out again and the dog was gone. He thought he was going crazy. Maybe it was the anxiety accumulated all those days with the threat of death hanging over him. Or maybe it was the pain that Camila's lie had caused him. Anyway, he didn't want to think about it anymore, he had to organize his ideas, keep his head clear. He had to promise himself to try to put the pain out of his mind, to put away that image that came back again and again, Camila's face, her eyes, her smile, to think clearly and to be able to face the danger. He had to remember that he was now alone. Alone. He took his last puff on his cigarette and put it out in an ashtray.

After giving an account of the meal and having a cup of coffee well charged with the intention of clearing himself to resume the journey, he paid and left the premises. He went to his motorbike and when he was about to get on it, he saw the dog looking at him again.

[

He was now on the other side of the road, his head sticking out through some bushes in a small grove along the road. He looked much more like a wolf now than he had before, perhaps he was. His eyes, grey and dark as the sky, twinkled for a few moments and then disappeared behind the bushes. Daniel noticed another sting in his hand and realized he had left the photograph on the table in the bar. Not that he cared much about losing it, but since he was there he went back inside to look for it. When he got to his place, he saw a waitress who was wiping down the table where he had eaten. She was not the waitress who had served him.

—Excuse me," he asked, "have you seen a photograph on the table?

The waitress, a forty—something, good—looking meat—eater, smiled at him and said:

—I can't tell you; everything is picked up with the tray. But come with me, please, we'll ask my partner.

Daniel accompanied her to the bar.

—I didn't really notice," said the bar manager. I've thrown away the trays that were brought to me. Wait a minute, I'm going to look through the waste...

Daniel was about to tell her it wasn't worth it, but she let him do it. After two or three minutes the waiter came back with the desolation drawn on his face.

—I'm terribly sorry," he excused himself, while I handed him the photograph, which had been split in two.

—Don't worry, it wasn't important," said Daniel, taking the two pieces.

He looked at the tomato and mustard stained surfaces. They probably would have torn the photograph in an oversight, next to the napkins or the paper tablecloth that covered the tray. His peaceful face in the middle of the dream had been torn in half.

[

Suddenly, he felt a chill run through his body as he remembered Mapuca's admonitory words:

When you break a photograph, you are destroying the receptacle of the person's soul and endangering his life... Then, by some strange association of his brain, the grey and fearful ones appeared again mentally eyes of the wolf watching him from the thicket.

CHAPTER 22

Nimp rove, but they also deteriorated as Daniel ot only did the weather conditions not approached his destination. It was as if heaven wanted to send him a message telling him not to go on, to turn around and walk away, that the place he was going to was where death was waiting for him. The darkness was intensifying as he went, and on the horizon the clouds were already as black as huge ink stains.

He could not take his eyes off the animal. In a way, it was a relief, because I didn't think about Camila that way. However, every time he imagined them shining in the darkness again, the restlessness took over more and more of his soul. He knew it was stupid, but it was impossible to stop imagining him as the reincarnation of Aukan. The look in that old Mapuche's eyes had become engraved in his mind. And so, had his words. Would it be true that he was worthy of death for something his company had done? He knew it wasn't so, that he had never hurt anyone and that he had no idea what was being done in his company. But was that an excuse? He remembered the phrase the old Mapuche had said to him: Isn't the shepherd responsible for what his sheep do? But the question was not that, but: what had the sheep done? The family business had been run by his father until his death, then by his brother, and when the latter disappeared, the responsibility was transferred to the management team, although his mother exercised certain supervisory tasks. When she died, the board of directors had offered him and his sister the management of the company, but both had refused. Daniel was not a person who could stick to the routines of a company, nor

[

did he wear a suit and tie every day. That would have made him feel caged in. He needed the air, the road, the freedom. Suddenly, a small animal ran across the road in front of him. Daniel tensed his muscles and held the handlebars tightly. He didn't try to brake, because he knew that, at that speed, it was easier for the bike to skid and he risked killing himself. Fortunately, the animal, which turned out to be a ferret, managed to reach the other side of the road. Even so, his body had been strained by the danger and his heart was racing. He took a deep breath to calm himself, and thought that the little animal had almost done the job of the witch—bird. That made him smile, but the smile faded from his face when the wolf's eyes reappeared in his mind. It seemed as if the beautiful and fearful animal had got into his head for some purpose. As if to warn him of something. Or as if it wanted to lead him through his mind to death. It made him think of the way the supposed witch bird had made the other partners in the conglomerate commit suicide. He thought it was silly to think that a simple mask had magical properties that would induce those who wore it to throw themselves out of the window. And he found even more absurd the story that the spirit of the witch—bird possessed them and forced them to do what he wanted. None of it made sense. But Aukan's words kept coming back to him, wise, terrible, accusing... He thought it was true that he had not dedicated himself to the company, that he had not wanted to confine himself to this life of paperwork and intrigues, that he had preferred the freedom of the road, the open spaces of the sea. But if he had been able to do that it was because he had his back covered, because he didn't have to work, or at least not regularly, because it was true that he attended some meeting from time to time, but it was more of a pose than anything else. Maybe the Mapuche

[

chief was right about that and he was like Alhué, the son of that greedy Indian named Hueicha, who destroyed the skin of the moon goddess to create his empire. And if he, like Alhué, enjoyed the benefits of his company, wasn't it also logical that he would answer for the damage it caused? But what was that damage? He thought he had to find out, and decided that as soon as he arrived in Santiago, he would go to the company's headquarters and investigate its activity in recent years. He didn't know how long it would take him to get it, because in fact he didn't know how long he had left to live, but he had to find out what that sin was for which the Mapuche spies were now demanding retribution. He remembered that Aukan had said that the amount that the gods had fixed the reparation was five souls. Not one less. And his own, his own soul, was the fifth. Then, a curious association of thoughts made him remember the meaning in Mapu—Dungún of the word
Alhué: 'lost soul'.

He continued on his way for a few more hours until he reached his destination. Once in the city, he headed for the northern area and finally reached the Great Santiago Tower, a structure almost two hundred meters high. In one of the last floors of that building was the headquarters of the family business. Daniel looked at the illuminated surface of the skyscraper. Although it wasn't yet dark, as he had left for the capital, the sky had become darker and darker. Looking at the building, he had the impression that this structure of steel, glass and concrete was the epicenter of the wrath of heaven, because the clouds that gathered over it were the blackest and darkest of all, and seemed to spread over the tower like the wings of a huge demon crow. Yet, like a strange omen, the rain still refused to fall.

He rushed up to the offices, where the employees they greeted each other warmly. His presence was not very common in that place, and even less so when he was dressed in jeans and a leather jacket, but he was the boss and, although he had never made use of his position to be treated in a special way, quite the contrary, he only found smiles painted on the faces of the staff. He felt sad and lonely. He realized that those smiles were not true, they never had been. Someone at the top could not expect sincerity from the people below him. He felt like never before a terrible desire to return to Camila, to embrace her, to believe all her lies and forget that she had cheated on him, to bathe with her again in the waters of Lake Villarrica and to make love to her again. Tears piled up behind his eyes, like rain behind the clouds, struggling uselessly to get out, because he, like the sky to rain, held them tightly. He took a deep breath and tried to overcome it, not wanting to give an image of weakness or eccentricity in front of his employees. He went to his office and asked the secretary to bring him all the files where the joint operations with the four companies of his partners that had been carried out in the last years were registered. She did not, of course, object, although she found the request made by her boss, late in the afternoon and dressed in that peculiar manner, strange. When they brought her several boxes full of documents, she ordered them to be put on her table and left alone.

He looked at those boxes with the same apprehension as he would have looked at a row of aliens. He had no idea where to start. It was beyond him. He had always been extremely lazy with paperwork. But he had to do it. Resigned, he looked out the window. The city at his feet was dark, only the lights of some buildings rose like ghostly figures surrounded by fog. He chose a

[

box at random, sat down and opened it. She started to check the papers, and after ten or fifteen minutes she realized that this was a titanic task. There had been many, many operations, but he did not have a clue as to what the madmen were accusing him of, so he could not see the matter. It could even be that very document he was holding in his hands at the time. He felt enormous frustration and lit a cigarette to calm his anxiety. The smoke spread through his lungs and caused him to cough. He thought he had to stop smoking at once, but it soon occurred to him that perhaps if everything happened as it seemed it would, this would be one of his last cigars anyway. In any case, he wasn't going to give up. He decided to start discriminating against documents. Although it was possible that by doing so he would inadvertently leave aside precisely the matter he was looking for, he did not have time for everything and needed to focus on operations that had something to do with the Araucania area. That was what he felt made the most sense. Then he realized that there was no point in going through files, but that he could make a first review of the data that was stored in the computer, and in a second moment he could get on with the paperwork. That discovery made him realize how clumsy he was in such matters, but it was a great relief to him. He went to his computer and turned it on. From his terminal he had to have access to all the information. Or so he hoped.

Suddenly there was a knock on the door and his secretary came in.

—They've brought a package for you," he said. The delivery man is downstairs, says he has to make the delivery by hand and requires your personal signature.

Daniel felt like his heart stopped. He had been waiting a long time to hear those words, so they didn't have to catch him off guard. But still, the knowledge that he had

[

arrived, that he was already there, somehow made all those fears that had haunted him the last few days come true. At last the witch—bird had decided to visit him.

—Let him come up, please," said Daniel.

When the secretary left the room, she took her mobile phone and dialed a number.

A couple of tones were heard and then a woman's voice answered.

—Hello, my boy," greeted Mapuca on the other end of the line. How are you?

—Mapuca," said Daniel, trying not to let the knot that had formed in his throat drown out his voice, "I'm calling you because the time has come?

—No!" cried the old nanny, who understood at once what was happening. Don't open it, my boy, don't open it!

—I have to, Mapuca," he replied at the edge of tears. I just wanted to talk to you. To hear your voice. I need to talk to someone I love before...

There was a silence on the other side of the line and then Mapuca asked:

—"What about Camila?

Daniel's voice got stuck in his throat when he heard that name. He couldn't go on talking.

—Daniel...?

—Listen, Mapuca," he said, trying to regain control, "don't worry, I'm not going to wear that mask.

—Don't open the package! —she repeated.

—I can't talk anymore...

—Where are you?

—I'm in my office.

—Call the police, my boy, please..." begged Mapuca in tears.

[

—What for? —Am I going to escape from these people like this? Aren't they going to send me more masks? I don't want to live under a continuous threat...

—I beg you, Dani... —She insisted.

There was a knock at the door.

—I have to go.

—I'm on my way, don't open the package until I get there," said Mapuca.

—I love you, Mapu," answered Daniel and hung up.

Mapuca, desperate, took her bag and ran to the street. As she walked to the taxi stand, she dialed a phone number on her cell phone.

After hanging up, Daniel thought about Camila again. He hadn't dared to tell Mapuca that he was out of her life. They called again. Absorbed in his thoughts and dejected, he went to the door and opened it. An employee of a transport company gave him a package wrapped in brown paper and a delivery note for him to sign as he received the shipment. As soon as he looked at the man, he took the pen and paper he had been given and signed. He didn't bother to look at the copy of the consignment he had been given; it would certainly be a false name. With the package in hand he went to the window. At his feet, the city was still seized by fog. When he heard the door close and knew he was alone he unwrapped the package and found a box exactly like the others he had received. Although he knew its contents perfectly, his hands began to tremble. Through the window he could see his image reflected against the background of the city in shadows. Absurdly, he imagined the wizard bird out there flying through the darkness, and that thought suddenly brought to his mind the name of Alhué, 'lost soul'. He knew that it was irrational, that in that box there was no spirit, that in fact the witch—bird didn't exist, that it was just an old wives' tale that could only scare impressionable people like Mapuca. However, if that was the case, why was it shaking? She barely gathered the strength to open the box, as her fingers barely responded. Once opened, he looked inside, and felt the blood stop in his veins as he watched the eerie gaze of the ro—ro bird. His sinister eyes, black as a deadly scorpion, seemed to rejoice that they had met at last. Something was calling Daniel from the box, or so it seemed to him, as if a voice from that object were calling his name. He didn't dare take off that red mask in the shape of an evil bird. Instead, he looked up and saw Santiago through the glass. In the midst of the darkness that enveloped everything, he thought he saw the steely eyes of the wolf sparkle, and at that very moment, a bolt of lightning tore through the night, illuminating everything. After a deafening thunderclap which seemed to be cracking the sky itself, the rain finally fell upon the city.

[

CHAPTER 23

You're not going to take it out

of the box? —

Daniel heard a voice behind him. He turned immediately and noticed that the delivery man hadn't come out when he closed the door. He looked at him in astonishment and indignation. He hadn't even noticed him when he handed him the package, as absorbed as he was in his thoughts. His voice was familiar, but in addition to being in the dark he had the visor of the jockey he was wearing down and he could not see his eyes. Then, trying to unravel his features in the gloom, he recognized the unpleasant moustache and could put a face to the voice.

—Cholo? —he said.

He looked up and let Daniel see his mocking eyes shining under the shadow of the visor.

—Did you miss me? —he asked, with that dismissive smile Daniel hated so much.

[

—Didn't you have enough? —he grunted, leaving the box on the table and turning to him in anger.

—Not so fast, little boy," said the Cholo, taking a revolver out of the pocket of his delivery suit and pointing it at the biker.

The biker stopped short when he saw the gun, and twitched his fists in rage. There was nothing he wanted more in this world than to wipe that smile off his face with one punch.

—What did you come here for? —He asked, "Are you the one who sent the packages?

—I am only the messenger, little boy," laughed the Cholo, scratching his jaw absently with the barrel of his gun. He seemed to be comfortable with guns.

—If you ever call me that again..." Daniel roared, taking a threatening step towards the other.

—What will you do then, little boy? —laughed the Cholo, pointing the gun at him again.

—Tell me why you have come," asked Daniel, breathing deeply and trying to contain the anger that was boiling in his body.

—I told you didn't know what you had done when you messed with me, biker," answered the Cholo with a hateful look. Now you will know.

Daniel said nothing, but he stared defiantly at his enemy.

—The truth is that I wouldn't like to be in your shoes

—said the Cholo, smiling again and approaching the table where the box was. Once there, he took the mask off and looked at it thoughtfully. I must admit it is frightening.

Daniel felt a chill when he saw that demon object outside the box. It was as if they had just taken a dangerous animal out of its cage. Cholo himself didn't

[

seem to have them all with him while he was holding him. He seemed mesmerized, as if the thing exerted some sort of influence on whoever was watching. He could not take his eyes off it himself.

—You're not going to tell me what you're doing here? —Daniel insisted.

—I came to make sure you put this on," said the Cholo, lifting the mask of the witch—bird slightly.

—And you think that if I wear it some spirit is going to possess me? —said Daniel, more to challenge the other than to make him laugh at the thought, which he found very disturbing.

—You shouldn't laugh at things you don't know," said the Cholo with anger in his eyes.

That seems to have hurt him, thought Daniel. If that guy was one of those religious fanatics who were so fond of such fantasies, maybe I could use that to his advantage.

—Correct me if I'm wrong," he said in a more relaxed tone. If I am not mistaken you want to be sure that I put on the mask so that the spirit which is enclosed in it can get into my head and force me to throw myself into the void?

—Smart boy, —confirmed the Cholo.

—But that plan lacks some legs," Daniel smiled.

—Yes?

—How are you going to make me wear it?

—Well..." sighed the Cholo with a face of annoyance, as if he were talking to someone incapable of understanding anything. Then, kissing the metal barrel of the gun, he added, "Maybe this one will give me a hand.

—You won't dare to shoot me," Daniel challenged him. As soon as the shots are heard, my employees will go in and call the police.

—Don't try my patience, biker," said the Cholo with a threatening look. There's nothing I'd like more now than to fill your body with holes.

—You know you're not going to shoot," said Daniel. If you kill me, I won't be able to put on my mask and throw myself out of the window, so that absurd rite of suicide won't happen. I don't think that's going to please whoever sent you. Which, by the way, who did?

—All in good time, my boy," said the Cholo, smiling once more. Daniel didn't like that smile at all, because it meant his enemy had some tricks up his sleeve. Indeed, after a few moments when he stared at him without stopping smiling, he added: "Now we're going to talk about your girlfriend...

Daniel felt his blood light up in his veins again and couldn't stop the other one from noticing how he was losing control. That obnoxious guy knew how to hurt.

—Don't bring her into this," he warned her.

—Sadly, she is in it now," said the Cholo with a satisfied look on his angular raptor's face. Even the locks.

—What do you mean?

—If I don't call a telephone number in half an hour and say a few key words, your friend will die.

Daniel felt the world crashing down on him. If they really had Camila, it was in their hands.

—How do I know you're not lying? —he asked in an attempt to reverse the position of power, which, at the time, was clearly in favor of the Cholo.

—Look," said this one, taking a piece of cloth from his pocket and handing it to him. Does that ring a bell?

It was the Mapuche flag on Camila's jacket. Someone had cut it, making sure to leave around a piece of fabric of the characteristic aquamarine color of the garment to prove its authenticity. Daniel could hardly hold back his tears, which he didn't know if they were from anger or from pain.

—That doesn't prove anything," he said desperately as a last resort.

—Maybe," admitted the Cholo boredly. But... you want to take a chance?

Daniel looked into his eyes desperately and, from the laughter he saw on his face, he understood that his enemy knew he had won. He couldn't understand why he was so vulnerable because of that woman. She was supposed to have deceived him, that there was nothing between them anymore. So why did he feel that he would rather die right there than have anything happen to her? Finally, he had to admit that there was nothing he could do.

—All right, you win," he admitted with an angry grimace. What do you want me to do?

—Good boy," said the Cholo, hiding the gun in his pocket and putting the mask back inside the box. Then he closed it carefully and handed it to Daniel, added: "Let's go for a walk.

Daniel took the box in his hands and followed his enemy. As they left his office, he felt as if what he was holding in his hands was a coffin, his own, and he had the horrible feeling that he and the spirit of the witch—bird that inhabited the mask would soon be one, and that they would both fly over the city that dark night.

CHAPTER 24

T he rain fell heavily on the roof of the Great Tower of Santiago. They had gone up to the top floor, where the belvedere was located, and then, behind a door to which the Cholo had a key, they entered a stairway leading to the top of the magnificent skyscraper.

—I see you're well organized," Daniel had told him as they climbed the stairs.

—You have to have friends in hell," was the other man's boastful reply. One of our contacts belongs to the team that cleans the windows of the building and provided me with a copy.

The temperature was cold upstairs and Daniel noticed a very strong air and had the feeling that the whole building was shaking. Although the heavy rain was wetting them, they were a little sheltered behind one of the metal structures around the top of the tower, because the rain wasn't falling vertically, as the wind was sweeping it away laterally. Anyway, he got the worst of it, because the other one had come with a raincoat to protect him from the rain. Daniel was grateful for the semi—darkness they were in, because it would probably prevent the Cholo from seeing that he was shaking. Although under normal visibility conditions you could see the whole city and the Andes from that place, that afternoon, surrounded by a thick blanket of rain and under a dark sky as if it were already dark, you could hardly see more than a few blurred spots around. In any case, it must have been about to get dark, although Daniel thought it impossible to add even more darkness to that terrifying scene.

[

—"Earlier, when we were going up, you referred to one of our contacts..." said Daniel, trying to stay away from the end of the deck. "Who are you?

—We? —We are the children of this country. The ones who lived here before you, and before people like you came to steal our land.

—Are you...? —Are you Mapuche?

—Does he miss you that much? —No.

—You seem... —I'm sorry.

—White? —Ironic Cholo finished the sentence. —I'm half—breed. My mother was one of you.

—I would never have said that," said Daniel thoughtfully, as he wiped the water from his face. The rain was lashing her body with powerful gusts and in a short time she had become soaked.

—You wouldn't have said that about Camila either, or about Thomas, would you?

—Not really," admitted Daniel.

—As you can see, appearances can be deceiving," laughed El Cholo, "but I think I'm getting too wet, so maybe we could just get it over with.

—At least tell me why you're doing this," Daniel asked.

—You want to know too much," said the Mapuche, glaring at his prey. Then, as if he was having second thoughts, he added, "The truth is that I'm enjoying this, so I suppose it's all right for me to give you an explanation. After all, you are going to take it with you when you fly. Daniel felt a chill when he heard those words, but thanked himself for the fact that the guy was willing to give him information. Not only because then he would finally know what the hell it all was about, but also because it would save him time.

—You must know that your girl, like me and a few others, belongs to a clan of agrarian Mapuche families under the authority of the great lonco Aukan," the Cholo began to explain. She and some of us are not pure Mapuches, but we do have some relatives attached to the tribe, and, whether for sentimental or cultural reasons, we feel attached to the group and maintain a close relationship with one another.

Daniel listened attentively to the Cholo's words, although he had to be especially careful to understand them because sometimes they got confused with the noise of the rain. The figure of the murderer, cut out by the dense layer of water and the ghostly lights floating on the roof of the gigantic building, looked unreal.

—As I have been told," he continued, "the lonco told you that about eighteen years ago there was a fire that destroyed many hectares of the Araucanía, our house... Daniel nodded his head.

—In that fire," continued the Mapuche, "not only were natural resources and vegetation devastated, but many animals died as well. But, besides, and this is what should matter most to you, little boy, Aimará, Camila's grandmother, died.

Daniel was amazed by that information; Camila had never told him anything about it.

—Aukan loved Aimara, he always did, since they were young. But she married a foreigner, a white man, Camila's grandfather. Even so, our lonco never stopped loving her. When she died in the fire, as my father told me, it was like her life was over for him. Since then, not a day has gone by that our old chief has not gone to mourn her in the forest, first over the charred remains of the vegetation, and then over the reforested area, where he had a shrine built in honor of his beloved. From the first moment, it was suspected that the fire had been

[

arson, and in time the police eventually confirmed this fact. However, the perpetrators could not be prosecuted because, although there were indications of who was responsible, it was not possible to gather sufficient evidence. Shortly after the fire, a regulation was adopted prohibiting the reclassification of burnt land for urban planning purposes in order to prevent arson for speculation on the land. Afterwards, everyone forgot about it, except our people, and above all our lonco, who patiently waited for years for the right moment when they could carry out their revenge. But to do so, he needed proof of who he was, and for a long time he did not find it. However, a few months ago, we discovered, a little by chance, that, more or less at the time of the fire, a commercial group tried by all means to prevent the approval of the regulation that prevented the urban rezoning. We investigated the matter and learned that this group had already tried to bribe the authorities when the draft land regulations were put on the table, that is, before the fire occurred. According to our information, it turned out that the people suspected of having caused the fire, to whom nothing could ever be proved, were people related to that business group. A trading group, which, by the way, consisted of five companies.

Do I need to tell you which ones?

Daniel didn't believe what he was hearing. He could hardly believe that the Cholo's words were true, because that would mean that his company, along with the other four that made up the business conglomerate, was responsible for that catastrophic fire and the death of Camila's grandmother. He barely noticed the water that fell heavily on him and he was soaked to the bone.

—No," he simply said to answer his interlocutor's question.

—Well," said the Cholo, satisfied. You seem to understand why you are here.

—You know I was only a boy then," said Daniel sadly. I wasn't even of age...

As he said this, he felt his heart filled with horror as he realized that, at the time of the fire, the one who was running the company was his brother Benjamin, five years older than he was.

—That's not relevant," replied Cholo. Through the mouth of the lonco, your priest, the gods are demanding the death of the five people in charge, one for each company, and today you are the top man in charge of your company.

After realizing that his brother, the person he had most admired in his life, could have been the cause of that horror —and all the circumstances pointed to that being so—, he thought that, in fact, it made sense that he should pay for it, that he should answer, not only for being the present owner of the company, but for being the brother of one of the authors of the fire. His death would finally close the circle. Tears flowed from his eyes and he did nothing to stop them, they were confused by the rain on his face anyway. He thought that, at that moment, the pain of the sky, which was throwing that flood over the city, was less than his own pain. He needed to know more, however, before he could face his destiny.

—What role did Camila play in all this? —she asked.

—We got down to business, eh? —laughed the Cholo. Then she looked at him as if she were considering whether to tell him or not. The truth is that she could tell you that she seeks revenge like all of us and that she wants you dead. I suppose it would hurt you

[

to know that she enjoyed deceiving you all the time, knowing that you were going to die...

—You're a scoundrel...

—But I'm not going to lie to you," continued the Mapuche without getting rid of his hateful smile as he spoke, "because I think the truth will hurt you even more. The truth is that it was a coincidence that we met that day in that roadhouse. When you walked into the place, Oscar recognized you. He knew you were one of the five who were receiving the boxes. Camila barely knew the story, although she knew that the lonco had ordered a retaliation against her grandmother's murderers, she was not aware of the details and, of course, she did not know that they were planning to execute the criminals. When we saw the box being delivered to you, Oscar and I

—We were very surprised; it was exactly the same as the boxes he sent us.

Daniel thought that confirmed the idea that they had nothing to do with the sixth box, the one containing the photos. Saddened, he thought he would never know what mystery they contained. At that moment he noticed again under his feet how the structure of the tower was shaken by the force of the wind, and the
terrible feeling of helplessness that

A chilling impression of vertigo joined in.

—When you left the premises, we told Camila who you were and asked her to find out how to follow you to find out what was in the box, so she went out and converted you. Then she managed to remove your lighter, which gave her an excuse to follow you and find out what we wanted to know without arousing suspicion. He simply had to say that he had found the lighter and had gone after you to return it, as he apparently did.

[

213]

Daniel thought he couldn't bear it any more, that he would almost rather put on the damn mask and end it all, because every word he was hearing that night from the Cholo was tearing his heart apart.

—It turned out that things did not go as planned," said the Cholo, unaware of the effect his words had on his interlocutor. That stupid girl fell in love with you. She had gone out with me a couple of times and I had been under the illusion that things could get worse, but you had to come along and spoil everything. —She gave Daniel a murderous look and paused, as if she had to make an effort to control herself. Then he continued with his story: "The worst thing was that when he heard about the plans for the Aukan, he threatened to tell you if we didn't leave you alone. He dared to say that he was capable of going to the police.

When Daniel heard those words, his heart seemed to explode, and he began to sob uncontrollably. He didn't care if that bastard saw him, he couldn't help it and didn't care either. He felt an overflowing torrent flooding his chest and the pain of the last few hours falling to his feet. The Cholo tried to hurt him by telling him this, but he had succeeded in doing the opposite. Daniel felt relieved. That terrible night, the last night of his life, he finally knew the truth. Then every gesture and word of his Mapuche princess took on meaning, and he knew that Camila loved him, and not only that, but that, despite appearances, she had done so in each and every moment they had been together.

—Will I have to call you a girl instead of a boy?

—The Cholo mocked when he saw Daniel crying. He did not answer, and the Mapuche, interpreting his tears as not relief but pain, continued to be satisfied with his story. That foolish woman needed to keep her mouth shut, so we had to take some measures that we did not

[

like at all, by order of the lonco. We held her mother and threatened to kill her if she told the police the story or if she told you the truth. Of course, we didn't intend to do anything to her. Aukan would never have attacked Aimara's daughter, but Camila was unaware of that.

Daniel thought that was the reason for the sadness he had detected when Camila talked about her mother. He felt that he would have liked to embrace her before he died, to tell her that he understood everything, that he didn't blame her for anything and that he only regretted not having known how to protect her better.

—The stupid woman thought that taking you out of the country would prevent us from coming for you. But unwittingly she ended up feeling helpless because we forced her to confess to us where they were going to go and then which hotel they were going to stay in Mendoza, threatening to make her mother suffer if she didn't tell us. It was a piece of cake for Oscar to get there and deliver the fourth package, in which we sent you the figure of the vengeful Pillán. It was burned as a symbol of the fire they caused.

—I didn't cause any fire," said Daniel.

—Save your excuses for those who want them," answered Cholo. Do you want me to finish, or do you want to take the leap now?

—Finish.

—Camila had the absurd idea of taking you to meet Aukan. She was convinced that the lonco, having met you, would have pity on you, that he would understand that you were not guilty of anything, as he told us. However, before going to the meeting, the lonco asked us to go to the place where they had met and discover it in front of you. We needed her to stay with us so that we could keep her later and use her as a bargaining chip so that you would agree to wear the mask. —El Cholo

[

215]

paused after those words and then added, "That reminds me, it is time to end the talk and get down to business. If you don't mind, little boy, the witch—bird is waiting for you.

Then, as if something had lit up in his head, Daniel looked at his enemy with an unexpected smile on his face and said:

—I'm sorry to disappoint you, Cholo, but I don't think I'm going to wear that mask today.

CHAPTER 25

T of the skyscraper, and at that phenomenal he rain and wind continued to sweep the roof height the swaying of the building's structure could be perfectly perceived. It seemed that they were on board a ghost ship hit by a storm in the middle of the ocean.

The Cholo looked at Daniel without fully understanding what those words were about. But he wasn't prepared to tolerate any games, so he took the gun out of his pocket and pointed it at the biker, he said:

—I think you're going to put your mask on.

—You're not going to shoot," said Daniel. That's not part of the plan and you know it. I have to kill myself.

—And what's changed now? —asked the intrigued Cholo. Do you care if we kill your girl?

—You gave me the key yourself to know that you won't," smiled the biker. —The Cholo stared at him blankly and Daniel added, "The lonco would never hurt Aimara's granddaughter.

The murderer's face filled with perplexity when he heard those words. Then he seemed to think for a few moments, and after that moment of doubt, he transformed his features into a hateful expression.

[

—Listen to me, little boy," he said, holding up his gun, "you are going to die tonight one way or another, you can be sure of that. Maybe you are right and the lonco would never hurt Camila, but I can swear to you that I would. If you put the mask on, it ends here. If you don't, I'll shoot you four times, and tonight I'll go to Pucón and shoot your girl twice in the head. It's up to you. But do it now, my patience is over.

Daniel looked into the Cholo's eyes and was sure he wasn't lying. That bastard would kill him and then kill Camila. It was at that moment, when he knew his time was up, that he noticed for the first time in a long time the box in his hands. Until that moment, he hadn't remembered that he was holding it, and now it weighed in his hands like a huge black rock, a magmatic rock, from the lava of a volcano.

—First do what you promised me," Daniel demanded.

—What?

—Call for Camila to be released.

The Cholo, while pointing at Daniel, took out his mobile phone and pressed a key. A number was automatically dialed and when someone answered on the other end of the line, he simply said before hanging up:

—"The witch bird flies once more.

Then he looked expectantly at Daniel with his calm, murderous eyes.

—I have done my part. Now it's your turn.

Daniel looked down at his hands. He felt his name being called out again from behind the lid of the box, and terror took hold of him. But he made an effort to control himself, he had to. He had to save Camila. It didn't make sense that they would both die. Before opening the box, he looked up and faced the Cholo again.

[

217]

—I know you believe in these things," he said. So, bear in mind my last words. If you touch one hair on Camila's head, I will come back from the grave to make you pay. That's a promise. Fear shone in the Cholo's eyes for a few moments, but then his haughty expression returned. Its owner nodded at the box, as if urging his victim to continue.

Daniel looked at the box again and lifted the lid. He was terrified and trembling, but he didn't know how cold it was that made him tremble, or how frightened he was when he saw those demon black eyes again. The raindrops fell on the red mask of the wizard—bird chirping on its lacquered surface. Daniel took it out of the box and held it in his hands. It was the first time he had touched the thing, and on touching it he felt as if a millenary current were running through his body. He knew that all this was suggestion, but he had the feeling that a demon was starting to take over his body. Could it be that which was making people commit suicide? Suggestion? Though the mask was light, it seemed to weigh like the earth itself, like a thousand planets together. He felt the weight of the mask in his hands pull him like an unprecedented tide, to a deep, dark place, perhaps even to hell, and he was sure that when he put it on, he would not hesitate for a second to throw himself into the void.

He slowly approached the end of the roof. All around him the rain continued to fall incessantly. He realized now that the Cholo had stopped talking, that the noise the drops made as they fell was deafening. As he approached the void, he felt the call of the abyss, as if the ground shouted out to him that it wanted to kiss him, that it wanted to embrace him, that it wanted to join him, with his bones splintered, his organs bursting against him, his blood scattered on its surface. It shouted to him

[

that it wanted to drink his blood, that it was thirsty for him, that there was only a short fall of three hundred meters and that the two would be united forever. Once he reached the edge of the tower, he looked down only slightly. Darkness enveloped everything, and he felt a deadly dizziness. His legs began to shake, and he had to make an effort not to fall before putting on the mask. That height, that verticality as sharp as the blade of an infinite razor, was almost impossible to bear. The ground was slippery from the water and the wind was pushing hard, and he had to hold on at the last moment to a metal cable that was attached to the rest of the structure to avoid falling. That move, however, caused the box to come loose from his hands and fall. Daniel saw that small object getting lost in the infinite, swallowed up by the shadows, just as he was going to do from one moment to the next. He heard again how something pronounced his name, and knew it was the mask he had in his other hand. His heart was pounding with unusual force and he found it difficult to breathe. He thought that he could not accomplish that, that he would faint before putting on the mask and fall from the building without having been able to fulfill his pact with the Cholo. He made a superhuman effort to continue. He had to save Camila. His last thought was for her.

At that moment, a bolt of lightning split the sky in two like the sword of a vengeful god and Daniel could once more contemplate the city, which glowed with the supernatural luminosity of that lightning that had fallen unusually close to him. He could also see the ground below and the cars driving in the rain like little insects moving frantically. He felt that his chest was going to explode. He was there, on the top of the world, almost touching the sky, next to the gods, who were bleeding their pain in the form of torrential rain and shouting their

[

anger in a voice of thunder. In that last instant he knew he was small, tiny, and felt all the force of nature roaring beside him ready to vent itself on him. The wind howled clamorously at his side, the rain beat down upon his body like millions of little darts, and he felt the charge of electricity in the air around him, like the deadly breath of a god. He looked at the mask in his hands, turned it over, and noticed that he no longer owned it, that his hands no longer obeyed him, and that the mask of the witch— bird approached his face to merge his spirit with his own and then to drag him along. He felt that he was getting dizzy and could hardly stand up, and in a last effort, which almost cost him what little energy he had left, he forced his lips to utter in a low voice a single word before the darkness took hold of him and his soul forever: Camila.

Downstairs, some three hundred meters away, Mapuca nervously urged the taxi driver to go ahead, but he told her he couldn't, that he was stuck in traffic. Maybe there would have been an accident a few meters ahead. Deses— parada, the Mapuche woman paid the taxi driver and got out of the car to walk. Under her umbrella she pantingly walked the distance from the Great Tower of Santiago. As she approached, she found more people in her way, and she had to get around them trying to reach her destination. When she was already in the vicinity of the skyscraper, her heart skipped a beat. The flashing lights of several police cars illuminated a crowd of onlookers piled up behind a police tape that cordoned off the area, blocking their way. In desperation she began to ask everyone if they knew what had happened, but no one seemed to know very well. Then she heard a woman about her age, a blonde, tell another woman that she was by her side:

—It was horrible!

[

Mapuca approached her and asked her with her eyes full of tears:

—What happened?

—It was horrible! —repeated the woman, who showed obvious signs of anxiety. I saw it. He fell in front of me and burst like a watermelon. It was horrible.

—What? Who? —cried a horrified Mapuca.

—I don't know," replied the woman, shaking her head. It was a man... All I could see was that terrifying thing lying there on the ground next to him.

—What... —What thing? —asked Mapuca, though he knew the answer.

—That... that mask... —It was on the floor full of blood next to the body and... what I saw... No, you won't believe me... Those eyes...

—What did you see? —Tell me, for God's sake! —pleaded Mapuca, holding on to the arm of that woman who was about to vanish.

The woman looked at her with eyes that reflected the fright and madness of someone who had just gone down to hell and seen Lucifer himself. The rain was falling hard on them, and that poor wretch took a few seconds to take a breath to respond.

—I had... I had the impression that that horrible thing was looking at me," he said at last, his face unhinged in terror. And then... I know it may seem absurd, but... I would swear... I would swear that he smiled at me.

CHAPTER 26

Accentuated dark circles under her eyes, to amila looked at herself in the mirror. which tears no longer flowed, as if all the tears she could shed had already come out, as if inside her there was nothing

[

left but a barren desert, unable to offer anything. She had spent the whole night crying. The call that the Cholo made to the lonco, uttering those terrible words, the wizard bird flying once more, meant that it was all over. He had tried by every means possible to prevent Aukan's terrible revenge from being fulfilled, but he had not succeeded. Now she felt broken, dead, empty. The rogue—smiling biker she had known only a week before had changed her life. From the first moment she saw him she realized that she connected with him and, as they became closer, she became aware that he was like a soul mate for her, with the same tastes, the same hobbies, the same way of facing life, the same passion. And little by little, without knowing how, she fell in love with him. With his gestures, his look, his jokes, his strength, his fragility, his love for freedom. And now... Now she could not conceive that she would never see him again. A deep, unbearable pain suddenly struck her, as if an enormous snake were wrapped around her chest, squeezing it until it broke her ribs, and she had to go back to bed so as not to fall to the ground in pieces. She opened her mouth and a scream tried to emerge from the deep pain that tortured her inside, but she did not succeed. She closed her eyes and squirmed on the bed with her mouth open, bending over like a wounded animal, trying to breathe, trying to cry, trying to pour out some of the poison that was killing her inside, trying to open a crack in that dark desert from which nothing could come out. At last a groan escaped from her throat and exploded again in a disconsolate, terrible, endless cry, like that of a little girl helpless in the dark. The tears were once again passing over the path they had travelled hour after hour in that long night, and Camila knew that the desert that was ravaging and burning her inside was unable to grasp them, she knew that Daniel's

[

fall, that devastating blow that had shattered him to the ground, had also opened a gap in his heart, a source in his heart that would never end. She cried and cried until she was exhausted, until her eyes hurt from shedding so many tears, and she fell asleep again.

An hour or two later, the cell phone vibrated in her pocket and the he woke up. He opened his eyes and returned once

more to reality, to that nightmare that would be his life from then on. He had put the phone on silent mode to get away from the world.

He looked at the screen and saw his mother's number. He'd been calling her all morning. And Oscar and Tomas. And probably all their friends. He looked at the missed call count and he was over 30. He hadn't answered any of them. They must have been worried about her, but she couldn't talk to anyone, she didn't want to. She just wanted to sleep. Disappear into the shadows, lose consciousness, cheat the pain. She remembered that when the Cholo had called, she had refused to believe that Daniel was dead, there was no room in her head for such a possibility. She also remembered that once Aukan knew that the command of the gods had been fulfilled, she allowed him to leave, and the first thing she did when the lonco men returned her phone was to dial Daniel's number, but he didn't answer. He didn't give a signal. It was as if it was disconnected or out of range. Or like he was torn to pieces when he fell in with his owner. He remembered that until he heard on the news that the businessman Daniel Balmaceda's had committed suicide he didn't believe it. Then she was broken, lost, as if floating on a thick cloud of pain, and without being very aware of what she was doing, she had gone to the small hotel in Pucón where they had slept the last time and had taken a room.

[

She had been locked up there since the day before, for more than twelve hours, and had not yet fully assimilated what had happened.

She remembered the last night at the lake, when she finally set aside

Fear, he removed the feeling of guilt, and let himself be carried away by his desire, for what he had felt from the beginning and had been repressing against the impulses of his heart. He remembered when he played that scene with Daniel in the hotel in Mendoza to get the truth out of the man in the yellow truck. And he thought that they both liked to play games and that they got on well together. He remembered their trips on the road, and the way they were both willing to give up everything to get on their bikes and heed the call of freedom. Then those strange words came to his mind that Daniel had spoken the night they were making love in front of the volcano. If I die, I will protect you wherever I am... I promise... She thought she really needed me to protect her now, to protect her from the immense suffering her loss had brought her, from the unbearable feeling of guilt that prevented her from emerging from that nightmare. All those memories were devouring her inside and it was so painful that she was sure that if the memory continued for a long time giving her teeth, she would end up losing all her flesh and becoming a mere ghost, a mere bone gnawed by suffering, a sad shadow of a woman.

He decided that he had to do something, that he couldn't go on like this, going around in that endless circle of misery. He washed his face and composed his appearance a little before going out into the street. She would go to a pharmacy and buy some anti—anxiety medicine or something that would take her away from that darkness which was blackening her soul more and

[

more and threatening to swallow her up and destroy her sanity. As she was leaving the hotel, the idea occurred to her that, little by little, over time, Daniel's face would become blurred, that he would end up forgetting his smell, his features, his voice. She didn't have any photographs of him, because he had kept his box. He didn't even have an article of clothing that would retain his smell. All that she had left of him was in her head and one day it would start to fade, it would gradually fade away, until it became unrecognizable. That idea seemed unbearable to him, and he had to make an effort to keep going. On her way to the pharmacy she passed by the bar where they had had breakfast the first time in Pucon and something pushed her in. She wanted to sit where she had sat with him. Breakfast she had with him. To hold on to her image in that place, to hold on tightly to her memory of him.

Sitting in the same place, she had the empty seat in front of her that Daniel had taken. The television was broadcasting the news as it did that morning they were there together and now, as on that occasion, they served him coffee too. The waitress was not the same. She was a Mapuche girl who he knew from his clan's environment and he had to exchange a couple of courtesy phrases with her, which cost him an unreasonable effort. He thought it was not a good idea to go in there. He glanced at the contents of his steaming cup, but did not taste it. He pushed it aside to make room so that he could rest his arms on the table and hide his face in them. It hadn't been a good idea to go out in the street, or to go into that bar. There was really no place to escape to, because her pain went with her everywhere, wherever she went. She felt like crying, but again the crying got stuck in her chest and this time, no matter how hard she tried, the tears did not come. They had stayed somewhere very deep in his

[

being, or they had simply run out. Perhaps this time his soul had dried up. She continued with her face on her arms, spilled on the table like a broken doll.

Then he felt something settle in his hair, and moments

Then he noticed a caress, a soft and warm hand was lavishing tenderness on him, but he did not obey his first instinct to turn around to see who he was. She felt that it comforted her, that in some strange way it took the pain away from her wounds. And she wanted to believe that that hand was Daniel's, who, as she told him, had returned from death to protect her. And that's why he didn't want to look, because he knew it wasn't his hand, because he knew that that hand would never caress him again.

—I've come to rescue my Mapuche princess from the volcano... When she heard those words she turned around, like lightning, because she knew that voice perfectly well and she needed to see that her head wasn't playing a trick on her. When her eyes saw his, contemplating her with that look that she thought she would never be able to see again, she felt her heart explode, she jumped up, embraced him like a madwoman, and then, finally, as if the world disappeared around her and a heavy chain broke into a thousand pieces in her inside, the tears came again.

CHAPTER 27

Camila thought that this had been a dream, as if t took several minutes for them to take off, as if she was afraid that, by stopping hugging Daniel, he would disappear. And he had missed her so much that he hadn't decided to let her go either. When he had been on the roof of the Great Tower Santiago had thought he would never see her again, nor hug her. Now, both seemed to be making up for the emptiness that had settled into their souls during the endless time they thought they would never be together again. Now and again they turned away from each other and looked into each other's eyes for a moment, but then they pressed against each other again, felt each other, made sure by the contact of their bodies that they were flesh and blood, that this was the truth. They needed all their senses to confirm what their hearts still doubted.

—I don't want to be a party pooper, guys," they heard after a while, "but the waitress is already starting to look at you in a strange way.

As if they had woken up from a dream, they unwrapped their embrace and looked at the person who had said that. He was a good—looking guy, tall, in his thirties or early forties, who looked at them with a smile. Camila had no idea who it could be, but suddenly something she saw made her say:

—I... I know you!

Then she looked at Daniel, who was looking at her with a smile full of happiness on his face.

—And how is that? —I want to know the stranger.

—Because of that cross that hangs in your chest... You are...

Benjamin?

[

—You were right! —said Benjamin to his brother. "This girl doesn't miss a thing!

—But... —How is it possible? —Camila asked Daniel, who she hadn't finished separating from.

—Now I'll explain everything to you," he replied, kissing her forehead, "but let's do it over a good breakfast, because the road, as always, has whetted my appetite.

They sat down and shared an exquisite breakfast. They needed to eat and get their strength back. They were exhausted but happy, as if they had just woken up from a nightmare and realized with relief that it had all been a bad dream, that the darkness in which they had been immersed was fictitious and the sun was shining in the sky.

Daniel told Camila that he had been calling her. She checked her cell phone and when she discovered among the missed calls that he had missed, she realized that if she had answered the phone instead of ignoring it, she would have been saved a lot of useless suffering. In fact, her mother and her friends had probably been calling to inform her that Daniel had not died. But... what had happened?

—How could he possibly...? —Mmm—hmm. — asked Camila, confused.

The television said that...

—I'm going to try to explain everything to you," smiled Daniel, pulling his hair out of her face, as he liked to do. ... Although I don't really know where to start.

—Then start from the beginning," said Benjamin, smiling.

Daniel explained to Camila that at the time of the fire in Araucania, his brother was the president of the Sociedad Balmaceda's, commercially linked to four

[

other companies, among which was Bildex, the company of Hugo Areilza, Andrea's father. In those years, Benjamin was quite inexperienced; he would not have been more than twenty—two or twenty—three years old, and quite a few things escaped him from the management of the company, in which, as he says, he had just landed. In any case, he was not unaware of the attempt by the companies associated with his to stop the enactment of a law preventing the urban reclassification of land destroyed by fire. When the fire in Araucania occurred, he had only to put the pieces together and realized that his partners were most likely behind it. His inquiries confirmed his suspicions and he was horrified to realize that if the law was not enacted, the business conglomerate would buy the land he had previously ordered to be burned and he would end up benefiting from a terrible tragedy. To prevent this, he spoke to the politicians responsible for the new law and informed them of the Areilza and his other partners' dealings. The evidence he had managed to gather suggested that they had bribed several of the people who had to vote for the law. He also went to the police and informed the investigators of his suspicions. Although, in the end, nothing could be proved, he did manage to get the law through, probably because of the fear of the politicians pointed out by Benjamin to vote against it, as this would confirm the suspicions they had. Regrettably, Areilza was not a man who easily forgave the grievances against him, and he swore to Benjamin that he would kill him and, if he could not do so, kill his family. Benjamin, although scared, did not take it too seriously, because he thought that Hugo Areilza was a businessman and not a gangster. Obviously, he was wrong; a person capable of setting fire to so many hectares of forest for

[

his own benefit was capable of anything. One day he received an anonymous phone call warning him that the brakes on his car had been tampered with so that he would suffer an accident. Probably the unknown informant was Areilza's own hitman, who did not want to have the young man's death on his conscience. Benjamin then realized that he was serious about this and that he could only end up with his death or, worse, that of his loved ones. So, he came up with a plan. He filled his car with half—empty beer cans and alcohol bottles and, after fixing the brakes so as not to have an accident while driving, he drove to a bend in a cliff and, after getting out of the car and realizing that he was alone, threw him into the sea with the windows open. The accident was simulated so well that authorities believed that Benjamin, under the influence of alcohol, had lost control of the car.

—After a long search, the police concluded that he had drowned and that the body had probably been carried away by the current at sea. Areilza, on the other hand, must have deduced that his plan had been a success and that his revenge had been consummated and that this made our family safe from possible reprisals. —At this point Daniel stopped his story to take a sip from his cup of coffee with milk.

Before it gets cold!

—And the photos... —What role do they play in this story? —I want to know Camila; whose curiosity grew as the story progressed.

—I was just getting to that," answered Daniel. Benjamin realized that if he told my sister and me or my mother that he was not dead, but was hiding in another country (he moved to Uruguay), he was taking a big risk. We would probably try to get him to come back, or

[

maybe we would go to the police to denounce Areilza... But without evidence, we would only make his sacrifice useless, because, warned, Areilza would try again to carry out his revenge, and, with Benjamin out of reach, the next victims would be us.

—Then he decided not to tell them anything," concluded Camila.

—Exactly," confirmed Daniel.

Then he explained to Camila that for Benjamin this separation was very painful, especially in relation to him, his little brother, whom he loved especially and whom he had always cared for and taught to move in life. He decided that someone had to know what had happened, but it could not be someone in his family or a person who could be under the threat of Areilza, although it had to be someone of absolute trust, and the only person who had these characteristics was Mapuca. So, before he put his plan into action, he communicated it to her, and although Mapuca tried to dissuade him at first, he finally understood that it was the least bad of the possible solutions, so he agreed to collaborate with him.

—Benjamin asked her to keep him informed of everything that was going on in our lives, especially in relation to me.

—Daniel continued. I wanted to know how I was growing up, if I was getting into trouble, if I had just been trained according to the teachings he had always given me. To do this, he also asked him to take pictures of me when I didn't notice, he wanted to see my face, how my features were changing, how I was getting along in life, etc.

—It was Mapuca who took the photos! —exclaimed Camila.

—Yes," said Daniel. Following my brother's instructions, he took pictures of me for several years, which he then sent via the Internet. In each of the photos, according to Benjamin's indications, he placed an object belonging to him (his old t—shirt, his lighter) in order to make it clear that he had had these photos taken, and that from a distance he cared for me and continued to look after me. He hadn't lost hope that he would one day be able to join us again, perhaps when Areilza died or so much time had passed that perhaps his desire for revenge would have passed. If that happened, he wanted me to have proof of his love, to know that he had abandoned me only to protect me, but that he was following me closely, even if he was in another country.

—You're going to get me all excited," Benjamin interrupted with a smile as he spread butter on one of the rolls he had ordered.

—You eat and let me finish the story," Daniel scolded amusingly.

—How the respect for the elders has been lost! — sighed Benjamin, and set about taking a good bite of his bread.

Daniel went on with his story and told Camila that Mapuca had done exactly what Benjamin had asked. Well, actually, not everything. Benjamin had instructed her to delete it each time she sent him an email with information about his family, so that no one would know that they were communicating. He also asked him to get rid of the photos after sending them by email, by deleting them from the hard drive and the camera he had taken them with. But she, superstitious as she was, made copies on photographic paper of all the snapshots. She feared, according to a Mapuche belief passed on to her

[

by her grandfather, that if the photographs were destroyed (even if virtually), the soul of the person photographed, who lived in them, would be damaged. By transmitting the soul of the virtual photographs to the paper copies, he was protecting, according to these ideas, Daniel's soul.

In all those years, Benjamin had only returned to Santiago once: on the day of his mother's funeral. He contemplated everything with tears in his eyes, from afar, but he did not dare to speak to Daniel or his sister, for it was dangerous, since Areilza had also attended the ceremony. Anyway, he hadn't changed his mind about keeping it a secret that her death had been faked.

—The truth is that when I was back in Santiago, I really wanted to go back," confessed Benjamin. I thought that, actually, if I was careful, it wasn't that big of a deal. I might even be able to make secret contact with my brothers again.

—But you didn't... —said Camila.

—No, I wasn't sure," said Benjamin. Well, the truth is that a couple of months or so ago I went back to Santiago. I decided to go alone for a few hours, and to meet with Mapuca before daring to see my brothers another time. I would discuss with her the possibility of coming more often to see my family. I thought that Santiago was a very big city and that after so many years I could move around in anonymity... How wrong I was!

—What happened?

Benjamin explained that when he returned to Santiago he met with Mapuca near where she lived, on the opposite side of the city from where Daniel lived. They hugged and cried together, and Mapuca explained to him in a loud voice all the things that had happened

[

in the family, although that information had been sent to him regularly in writing. When he confessed that he had kept the photographs on paper, Benjamin was frightened. Probably absurdly, because those photos didn't have to mean anything, but he didn't want there to be anything that, even remotely, could be associated with his being alive. She begged him to take them, promising him that he would keep them without tearing them up, and that from then on he would make paper copies of all the photographs he sent her and keep them intact. Mapuca went to get the photographs from his house and took them to Benjamin. He said goodbye to her and went to the airport in Santiago to take a plane to Montevideo. As he arrived too early, he went to the cafeteria to have a drink to kill time. But bad luck wanted Areilza to enter the cafeteria as well, since he was at the airport on a business trip. When she saw Benjamin, she couldn't believe her eyes.

Benjamin Balmaceda's was alive! When Daniel's brother saw his enemy, he left the cafeteria in a hurry, guided by one of his henchmen. Although he managed to get away from him, he realized that he had left the photographs on the table in the bar.

—And how did they end up getting to you? —Camila asked Daniel.

—We're not sure about that anymore," said Benjamin for his brother, "but we think Areilza found the photos and must have wondered what I was doing with some photos of my little brother. She probably assumed that he knew I was alive and thought he was in contact with me. The best way to find out was to follow him. Maybe he did that for several days, and when he saw that he wasn't with me, he decided to force him to make a false move and set up some bait. Since he had

[

received, like the other partners, several packages from an unknown sender, he must have come to the conclusion, correctly, that Daniel was receiving them too. So, he sent him the photographs in a similar box (he probably used one of the ones sent to him). If, as Areilza thought, Daniel had a relationship with me, he would be very surprised and would want to understand what the relationship was between those photos and the other boxes, so he would contact me and try to find out. That would be the moment when Areilza would take the opportunity to hunt me down.

—That's why he had you followed by the guy in the yellow truck...

—concluded Camila, addressing Daniel.

—Exactly," confirmed this one. At least that's what we think.

Camila stayed meditating for a while. That shed light on the mystery of the photographs. All the pieces of the puzzle were fitting together. In that story lay probably the pain that she had detected in Mapuca the day they met, just as the old Mapuche woman had suspected that she was also keeping a secret.

—And didn't Mapuca warn you that Daniel was receiving some strange packages? —he asked Benjamin.

—Yes, of course," he answered. When she spoke to you and you told her, she called me. That's when, in relation to each other, I imagined what had happened. On the one hand, I assumed that Areilza was sending the photographs with the purpose that we had just exposed to you, and on the other hand, thinking about the matter, and thanks to the information that Mapuca gave me, I realized that behind all that must have been the revenge of some of the victims of that terrible fire that happened so many years ago. I decided to investigate on my own and asked Mapuca to keep me informed if there was any news. Of course I did not return to Montevideo, but stayed in Santiago, staying in a hotel located in the Providencia neighborhood, halfway between Daniel's apartment and the World Trade Center Santiago complex, where our company is located; that way I could keep a close eye on my brother and protect him in case of need.

—It really seems like a crazy story," laughed Camila, as she held Daniel's hands affectionately. But I still don't know how you escaped death...

—Well, if I have to tell you the truth, it was a close call —he smiled. Well, more like a phone call.

—A phone call?

—Let me explain... —I suppose you know that the Cholo came to visit me...

—Yes, I know," she said, letting a shadow cloud her pretty eyes.

—Don't be sad," said Daniel, when he detected that expression on her face. I know you had nothing to do with it. That guy told me everything.

—I'm surprised he did, she said. He only wanted to hurt you...

—I think that's precisely why he did it. He must have thought that if he told me the truth (that you not only hadn't been involved in this, but also tried to save me), I would suffer more knowing that you really loved me, but I could never see you again.

—He's a pig," she said.

Daniel looked at her and realized that he didn't know the whole story yet.

—He came to visit me," she continued, "and forced me at gunpoint to follow him to the roof of the

[

skyscraper. Then he threatened to kill you if I didn't put on the mask, which I had to do.

—Did you... put it on? —asked Camila, frightened.

—I was about to do that when suddenly I heard a voice calling my name. I looked at the place from which it came and almost fell from the building of the impression. There, in front of me, was Benjamin! The brother I thought was dead!

—You should have seen the look on your face! —Rio the alluded one.

—Don't laugh, you scoundrel, I was almost scared out of my wits! —Daniel laughed in turn.

—And how did you know I was there? —Camila asked Benjamin.

—When Mapuca left the house to go to the company to meet Daniel, he called me, just as I had asked him to," answered Benjamin. Besides, she lived on the other side of town, so it would take her a long time to get there, and I could be there in ten minutes.

—That's the call I meant," added Daniel.

—And the Cholo?

—He was on the ground, half unconscious," said the biker. There was a huge storm, and, with the noise of the rain, I didn't hear my brother arrive and face the Cholo. As he told me later, they had forced it and at last he had managed to reduce it. Then he took the gun away from him...

—But... on TV they said you were dead...

—she interrupted.

—Yes..., it was all a confusion. And now comes the strangest thing in history," said Daniel. When I hugged my brother, I was in shock. He told me to get out of there, that he would explain everything to me in front of a

[

whisky, that I needed to dry and warm up or I would catch pneumonia.

—You were blue," confirmed Benjamin, "I don't know whether it was the cold or the fear...

—I'm not afraid! —protested Daniel.

—Well, whatever it was," said his brother, "you were soaked to the skin.

—When we passed by the Cholo we saw that it was coming to life," Daniel continued, "and Benjamin decided to call the police. But first, a little as a joke, he put the mask of the witch—bird on him...

Camila's eyes opened like plates. That face of perplexity and the dark circles under her eyes didn't make her look her best, but even in those circumstances, Daniel thought she was beautiful.

— I was scared too when I saw him do that, he said. The truth is that I had started to be afraid of that damn mask...

—Didn't you say you weren't afraid? —Benjamin scoffed.

—Maybe it would have been better if you'd stayed in Monte—Video," joked Daniel.

—Then who would have saved you, little brother?

—Are they always like this? —asked Camila, smiling.

—I don't really know how we get on," said Daniel. We haven't seen each other for many years...

The smile faded from Camila's face, as if it had been a mere excuse to put her fear aside for a moment.

Then, returning to the worried gesture that had preceded it, she asked:

—And what happened next?

—That's the strange thing," said Daniel. The Cholo seemed to go mad. He stood up as if out of his mind. And he screamed like a condemned man, as if all the

[

demons in hell were chasing him. And then... then he jumped off the tower without my brother or I am being able to stop him.

Camila remained silent for a moment. She seemed to be assimilating what she had just been told. Then she said:

—"He deserved it, but I can't help but shudder...

—I understand," said Daniel sympathetically. It was a brutal fall.

—And how is it possible that the television... —

—Well, maybe it was our fault," explained Benjamin. My brother was shaking so badly that instead of going straight to the police, I walked him home, which, as you know, is very close. We weren't there long, just long enough for him to take a hot shower and dry himself off. Then I made him some very hot rum and milk to help him recover and told him what had happened and why he was still alive. When we finally went to talk to the police, information had leaked out to the media. The inspector handling the suicides had contacted the CEO of our company to warn him of the danger...

—But it's not Daniel? —interrupted Camila.

—No," he said, "I'm actually the chairman of the board of directors, but as I hardly ever go to the meetings, and delegate everything to the director, it was the director who kept in touch with the police. In fact, he didn't even think it was necessary to say anything to me because they took it for granted that I wasn't the person being threatened.

—Above all because you didn't tell him you had received the packages either, nor did you go to the police," Camila scolded him.

—As I was saying," Daniel continued, without taking any notice, "when he heard about the new suicide, the

[

inspector went to the company and there my secretary told him I had gone up to the top floor, but that she hadn't seen me come down again.

—We went straight down in the elevator without going through the company first," said Benjamin.

—Then the inspector imagined that it was me who had fallen," Daniel continued, "because that seemed to follow the pattern of the other deaths and confirmed his suspicions that a director of our company (although he thought it would be the CEO and not me) would be the next victim.

—Of course, it was only a police hypothesis," added Benjamin, "and it couldn't be verified until the coroner checked the identity of the dead man. But you know how these things are... Information is immediately leaked to the press, and since this hypothesis was practically taken for granted by the police, the television broadcast it without checking it...

Camila then thought that, in reality, the announcer had not literally said that he had died, but rather that "reliable sources indicated that the victim was the businessman Daniel Balmaceda's...

—When we finished testifying to the police, we went home," said Benjamin. We caught up with our lives and then decided to get some rest, because we were exhausted. But we couldn't sleep more than a few hours, because here your friend, not being able to reach you by phone, decided that he would come looking for you directly. He said something like he was able to turn the whole Araucania upside down until he found you!

—You really said that? —I did. —Camila asked Daniel, feeling that the emotion was overflowing.

[

—All that's left is for you to support him! —Benjamin joked, "Do you know what time we got up to come here and find you?

—And how did you find me?

—It was a bit of a coincidence,' said Benjamin. Daniel didn't know where you were, but from what the Cholo told him he assumed you were somewhere near Pucón, which was where the kidnappers had apparently kept you. And since my little brother is very intuitive, he had a hunch and decided that we should go to the hotel where you stayed once here. On the way, we passed this bar, and Daniel looked through the window, and when he saw you, he almost kissed me with the joy he got!

—You're exaggerating! —Rio Daniel.

—Well, I think you're all crazy. —I'm about to go back to Montevideo and stay there! —joked Benjamin.

Then something seemed to break into Daniel's mind and made him adopt a serious expression.

—Is something wrong? —asked Camila.

—There's one thing that worries me," he answered. It's something I don't understand...

How could a simple mask force the Cholo into the void...

—You never did stop believing in the witch bird, did you? —said a deep and unexpected voice behind them.

The three boys looked at the place where that voice came from and found themselves with grey wolf's eyes, which both Daniel and Camila knew very well.

[

CHAPTER 28

S sat up in his   seat, driven by rage. Camila held eeing the man who had tried to kill him, Daniel

his arm and he, holding himself back, sat down again. The log came to the table and said:

—"I see that, as I was told, the witch—bird made a mistake in his flight this time.

—What do you want? —asked Daniel dryly.

—That's not the kind of manners I expected from your friend

—said Aukan, looking at Camila. Aren't you going to invite this old man to sit down?

Daniel and Camila exchanged a look, and Camila invited the Mapuche chief to sit down at the table with a nod. Then she asked:

—How did you know we were here?

—It's an advantage of age," said the lonco. Over the years, although you lose your sight and hearing, you accumulate ears and eyes everywhere.

The expression on all three of them implied that they did not understand what he meant, so Aukan pointed to the bar, where the Mapuche waitress greeted him with a respectful head bow.

—You are a criminal, Aukan," said Daniel, "and a vengeful old man.

—The gods required five souls in atonement," said the old man as an excuse. His wolfish eyes looked more tired, as if they had grown old since Daniel last saw them.

—Do you mean to say that you still persist in the idea of killing me?

[

—asked the biker, twitching his fists and setting a threatening tone to his question.

—The account has been settled," Aukan replied without hesitation. Five souls have been delivered, though none of them were yours.

Camila seemed to breathe a sigh of relief at the sound of it. That meant that the Mapuche condemnation that weighed on Daniel's head no longer existed.

—What... —What power does that mask have? — Daniel suddenly asked. He had asked that question almost without realizing it. He didn't want to talk to that man, he didn't want to give him the pleasure of being weak in front of him. But he needed to know if it was only suggestion that had made him feel dominated by the spirit of the witch—bird, or was there something else? He needed to push aside the shadow that was still woven into his thoughts.

—For our tradition," Aukan answered, "the warlock bird dwells in it, and he who wears it is possessed by it.

—I know," Daniel became impatient, "but is that all?

—You wonder why the one who wears it seems to be in love with it. I think, after what has happened, you have a right to know the reason. —The lonco looked vaguely at the snake shape carved on his stick. There is a poison in a Mapuche plant, whose name I will not reveal to you, because it is only transmitted from machi to machi, which is what we call our medical advisors, or, as you would call them, shamans?

—A drug? —I want to know, Daniel.

—Let's say it's something you can't buy in a supermarket, although, yes, we could call it that," answered the lunco. That... drug produces a hallucinogenic effect, similar to a bad LSD trip, and the person who takes it starts to get delirious and, if he is at

[

a considerable height, it is natural to go into a vacuum. Maybe thinking it's a bird. Maybe trying to escape from that bad feeling he's got in his head. Who knows? We impregnated that substance into little spikes which were in the mask, and the one who put it on immediately suffered the effects of madness, which passed from the skin of the witch—bird to travel through the veins of the wretched man. To give you all the information you need, I will tell you that it is an undetectable substance, in the unlikely event that someone should think of doing an autopsy on a mangled body, the cause of death of which is obvious. All we needed to do was given a little push to the person who was to wear it to do it. And that little push was provided by the Cholo, either by intimidating the condemned person or by blackmailing him with harming a loved one.

Aukan seemed to be moved by those last words, and needed to get some air before adding:

—"I feel responsible for what happened to that poor boy...

—You're a murderer! —said Daniel again, as he felt the rage coming back. I should turn you in to the police.

The wolf's eyes became opaquer, glassier, but they didn't reflect anger or insolence, but a strange and intimate regret. He twirled his carved wooden stick between his fingers and said:

—You are right.

Daniel and Camila looked at each other, and Benjamin himself seemed surprised by that answer. The lungo continued:

—You don't have to give me up, because I'm going to do it myself.

[

Camila, amazed, was going to say something, but the lonco stopped her with a gesture of his hand and continued talking to Daniel.

—I could beg you to forgive me, but I won't. What I have done is unforgivable, so I am not going to ask you for it. But instead I'm going to tell you briefly a story that wasn't so short, but too long. The story of a heart.

Aukan took out a wooden pipe and a small metal box from his pocket. He took a couple of pinches of tobacco from it and carefully placed them in the bowl. His winged fingers, slightly deformed by osteoarthritis, handled the sting with extreme delicacy, gently tamping down the strands to allow them to breathe. The three young men watched as if hypnotized by the activity of the old man. He took the pipe to his mouth by holding it by the bowl and lit it. The aromatic smoke of tobacco enveloped his face for a few moments. When this little ritual was over, he spoke.

—The heart that holds my chest still beats, though it should not. It is a very old heart, but it was not always so. At one time he was young and fell in love with a beautiful woman, so beautiful that her eyes, which changed like the sky itself throughout the day, seemed to direct the music of the stars. That gift was passed on to his granddaughter, who now sits beside you.

—Aukan pointed with his sad eyes at Camila, and then lost his gaze somewhere beyond the walls of that room and far from the time in which he found himself. He gently sucked in the smoke of his pipe, held it in his mouth for a while without giving him access to his lungs, and let it go languidly before resuming his story. The woman did not reciprocate, and the young heart suffered its first wound. It would be a wound that would never close, because from the moment he met her, she was

[

the one who gave continuity to his beating, so that that heart knew that it would stop if one day, even from a distance, he stopped seeing her. That day came, because she was taken from him by a fire caused by the greed of the white man. And that second wound was even more devastating than the first. However, the gods sent him the greatest punishment, perhaps for daring to love something that only belonged to them: they punished him to keep on beating. And he had to beat for many more years, pumping out increasingly black blood. And the pain gangrened the heart, which gradually corrupted and rotted, pushing away with each beat all the good and tender things that once inhabited it. And love was replaced by fury, and the rot emitted its effluvium from the chest upwards, clouding the poor head and filling it with madness

The three of them listened to the old man's words attentively. Daniel, listening to the story of that old heart, could feel in his own heart how the feelings fought against each other. On the one hand, he hated the man who had inflicted so much suffering on him. On the other hand, he pitied the old man before him, whose eyes were no longer those of a proud wolf, but those of a poor old man worn out by years, by hatred and by pain. An old man who, from what he was telling, had actually been dead for a long time.

—Mary was my ear today," he said, nodding to the Mapuche waitress, "She told me, from what she heard of your conversation, that you," he said to Benjamin, "were not only not responsible for the fire, but that it was thanks to you that the law safeguarding our lands was passed. Perhaps without your help, part of Araucania would now have been urbanized and invaded by cement and asphalt. And I...

[

—His voice trembled and seemed to be stuck for a moment, until it started again weakly.

—Lonco..." said Camila, pitying the old man who seemed to have no strength left to speak.

—No," Aukan stopped her and waved his tired hand at her. Please, I beg you to spare me the humiliation of pity. I deserve neither your pity nor your forgiveness. I'm sorry, white man," he said to Daniel. I am sorry for the pain I have caused you... you and your brother. You are both pure souls, and I have made you suffer unjustly, blinded by hatred.

He then looked at Camila with infinite sadness in his grey eyes and added

—"I feel especially sorry for you, Aimara's granddaughter. Shame and disgrace will be with me until the last day of my life, which I hope will come soon.

With those words, Aukan rose slowly and leaned on his wooden staff, followed by the smoke of his pipe to the door. He opened it and left the premises hunched over and defeated. That was the last time he would be seen. But the three of them sensed that whoever came through that door was not a man, but a destiny. The destiny of someone who one day was a proud
Mapuche chief, condemned to live a life he would never have chosen, and of whom there was nothing left but an old shadow. The long, sad shadow of a mortally wounded wolf.

EPILOGUE

Twere a huge blue —winged butterfly flying he sky stretched out before his eyes as if it towards immensity. The clouds, white as freshly washed, piled up on the horizon in puffy cumulus clouds, adopting curious shapes, which evolved with the whim of the wind and reflected the soft sunlight on their cottony surface. The mineral voice of the earth welcomed the bikers once again, rejoicing that they were to be seen again and that they were to caress their old skin with their wheels once more. Benjamín had stayed in Pucón; for him, a new trip was very tiring, and it had been many years since he had been in that small town, so he decided to stay a couple of days and enjoy the beauty of the Araucanía. Camila and Daniel were no less tired than he was, but what they needed now was something else, and they both knew perfectly well which one. To ride together once more on their motorcycles, with no other destination than their hearts and the road pointing to them. It didn't matter for how long, an hour, two, three... They just needed to do it.

Daniel saw his biker girl in front of him again, as right—handed as a Mapuche horse on her metal horse, letting herself be carried away by the road once more, as her song said. And this was the first time he didn't feel afraid, when not only did an endless road of asphalt lie before him to be travelled alongside it, but a whole lot of days, months, years, without that shadow that used to accompany them and that threatened to end everything at any moment. Now there was only light, a radiant and pure light that cleared the darkness from the road and illuminated the route.

Bikers passed on the other side of the road, and he and Camila responded to their greeting by placing their hand at the knee in a V—shape. The smells that the road brought with it, seized him again. The smell of the meadow, the manure of the fields, the fragrance of the trees... He knew that, at that moment, there was only one place in the world that he wanted to be, and only one person with whom he wanted to share it. And that place was where he was now, wandering on the asphalt with his Mapuche princess. How much he had needed that! To run away with Camila, to get on his motorbike, to ride far, far away, to the end of the world, and to get lost there with her. And the wind, once again the wind, surrounded him with its vigorous embrace, until it melted with him and disappeared, transforming itself into a light breeze, almost imperceptible, just like it happened to the road and to the motorbike itself, his girl, his wonderful midnight star. Everything would disappear, dissolve with speed and become one with him, and he himself would stop being him and become part of the road. He held the handlebars of the bike firmly in his two gloved hands. The spider's bite had healed and, like the witch—bird, had disappeared forever from his life.

The road had been long and hard, but the bad had been left behind. The noise of the engine caressed his ears, and he let himself be carried away once more by its whispering and by the music of the asphalt that he and Camila composed as they rolled. Everything seemed to have gone wrong. His brother had returned from the dead. He had saved her life. And above all, Camila loved him, and they were together again. There were no more masks, no more packages, no more anger from the volcano. He looked again at the expanse of light that opened up before him and gave thanks to heaven.

[

And, not being sure to whom it would reach, he lifted a small prayer to the heights. All he asked for was time to spend with the woman, life to travel the roads, and a good ear to be able to continue listening for many years to that distant and echoing call, which once answered cannot be forgotten: the call of the road. A call that the wind carries to a thousand places, but only a few chosen ones, very few, can hear.

THE END

www.ingramcontent.com/pod-product-compliance
Lightning Source LLC
Chambersburg PA
CBHW020908160726
47993CB00005B/1873